To Grandmother's House We Go

BOOKS BY WILLO DAVIS ROBERTS

To Grandmother's House We Go

Willo Davis Roberts

Aladdin Books

Macmillan Publishing Company   *New York*

Maxwell Macmillan Canada   *Toronto*

Maxwell Macmillan International
New York   Oxford   Singapore   Sydney

To my granddaughter,
Samantha Roberts

First Aladdin Books edition 1994

Aladdin Books
Macmillan Publishing Company
866 Third Avenue
New York, NY 10022

Maxwell Macmillan Canada, Inc.
1200 Eglinton Avenue East
Suite 200
Don Mills, Ontario M3C 3N1

Macmillan Publishing Company is part of the Maxwell Communication Group of Companies.
Printed in the United States of America
10 9 8 7 6 5 4 3 2 1
A hardcover edition of *To Grandmother's House We Go* is available from Atheneum, Macmillan Publishing Company.

The Library of Congress has cataloged the hardcover edition as follows:
Roberts, Willo Davis.
    To Grandmother's house we go/by Willo Davis Roberts.
    — 1st ed. p. cm.
"A Jean Karl book."
    Summary: To avoid foster-home care while their mother is recuperating from an illness, three children run off to the home of a grandmother they have never seen, where they find a cold reception and a terrible secret.
    ISBN 0-689-31594-5
    [1. Mystery and detective stories.   2. Brothers and sisters—Fiction.
3. Grandmothers—Fiction.   4. Pyromania—Fiction.] I. Title.
PZ7.R54465To 1990 [Fic]—dc20
89-34972
ISBN 0-689-71838-1 (Aladdin pbk.)

1

ROSIE WAS JUST DRIFTING OFF TO SLEEP, thinking of the cocker spaniel puppy she was hoping to persuade her mother to allow them all to have when she came home from the hospital. It would be a soft, reddish-blond little creature that would wag its tail whenever it saw her and lick at her chin when it crawled into her lap. Rosie smiled as if it were already happening.

Without warning, a cold hand was clamped around her wrist, jerking her out of the half-dream, wide awake.

"What—Nathan, you scared me!"

"Shhhh!" Her eight-year-old brother stood beside her bed in his pajamas, silhouetted against the light that came past her bedroom door from the night-light in the upper hallway. "Don't make any noise," Nathan cautioned.

There was no mistaking his voice. Her brother Kevin said Nathan sounded like a frog with a sore throat and looked like an owl with his horn-rimmed glasses.

Nathan wasn't wearing his glasses now; somehow he looked smaller without them. "Come on," he said, turning away.

Rosie made a grumpy sound. "What for? I was just starting to have a nice dream—"

"Shhhh!" Nathan said again, more fiercely this time. "Pay attention."

Rosie was two years older than Nathan, but sometimes she felt as if he were her grandfather. Her annoyance subsided now that she was fully awake. Nathan wasn't one of those pesty little brothers. There must be something important going on for him to speak this way. She sat up, sliding her feet over the edge of the bed. "What's the matter?" This time she, too, whispered.

"Mrs. Kovacs called Aunt Marge," he said. His brown hair stood in untidy tufts, and his dark eyes looked big and naked without the familiar lenses. "She asked her to come over for an emergency consultation."

Rosie slid out of bed and, without bothering about slippers, padded after him onto the second floor landing. "Emergency consultation?" she echoed. "About what? Is Mama worse?" Alarm twisted at the pit of her stomach.

"I don't know," Nathan said, "except that it's about us. Kevin heard Mrs. Kovacs talking, and she sounded upset. Kevin said to tell you to come. We have to listen when Aunt Marge gets here."

Rosie looked up at the clock on the landing, the grandfather one that had belonged to Mrs. Kovacs' mother. "Aunt Marge is coming over here at ten o'clock at night? What are we going to do, eavesdrop?"

"It's the sensible thing to do, if it's about us," Nathan said. "Come on."

Nathan was almost always sensible. She followed him, bare feet making no sound on the hardwood floor, to find Kevin at the head of the stairs. He was only a year and a half older than Rosie, but he was much taller, and skinny. He, too, wore pajamas, and he gave the other two a look that Rosie knew meant they weren't to speak.

There was a light on in the living room downstairs, and the sound of the television. Surely it couldn't be anything too terrible, Rosie thought, or Mrs. Kovacs wouldn't be watching television. Yet her heart had begun to thump under her ribs. So many rotten things had happened lately, and she prayed there wasn't going to be another one.

Unexpectedly, voices drifted through the kitchen doorway that was almost beneath them, sort of tucked under the stairs. Nobody was watching TV, then. The pressure in Rosie's chest increased, though she couldn't have said why.

"If it's as serious as you say, of course I don't mind coming out at night." Aunt Marge, their mother's older sister, had already arrived.

Something clattered, as if Mrs. Kovacs had put cups into saucers. Rosie's mother said Mrs. Kovacs was the only person she knew who still used cups and saucers instead of mugs. Rosie stepped to the railing and leaned out, the way Kevin was doing, to hear better.

"Well, it sounded serious to me," Mrs. Kovacs said.

Rosie couldn't see her, but she knew exactly how Mrs. Kovacs looked. She was short and stout and always wore a voluminous apron—today's was a pink and red print—over an old-fashioned housedress. She wore comfortable shoes because she had bunions, which were nothing like the *onions* Nathan had originally thought she'd said, but some sort of bumps that hurt her feet. She had gray hair fastened somewhat untidily in a bun at the back of her head, and a jolly pink face.

Right now she didn't sound jolly at all.

"Who did you say you talked to at the hospital?" Aunt Marge asked, and Rosie's stomach tightened even further.

It *was* about Mama, then. And it was serious. For a moment Rosie's knuckles grew white as she gripped the banister.

"That Ms. Hayboldt," Mrs. Kovacs said. They heard the scrape of the teakettle as it was replaced on the gas burner. "Help yourself to sugar, Marge. You know the one. You can't tell if she's married or single, calling herself *ms.* that way."

"I don't suppose it matters to anyone but her," Aunt Marge said calmly. Aunt Marge often got mail addressed to Ms. Marjorie Woodruff; Rosie had seen it. "She's in social services. How come she's reporting on Lila's medical condition? Usually they don't let anyone but doctors do that, not even the nurses."

"Well, she wasn't exactly telling me about Lila's condition. She sounded flustered when I didn't already know, but then since she'd already spilled the beans she said what she called for. That Lila is probably going to have to be in a nursing home for quite a while. Months, she said."

Rosie let out a little of the air she'd been holding. Months more in the hospital, but at least Mama wasn't dying. Since Daddy'd died, Rosie had thought about death a lot.

Aunt Marge sounded thoughtful. "It creates some new problems, all right. You've been wonderful, taking in three kids who aren't even related to you the way you did. Of course neither of us thought my sister would be in the hospital for ... what's it been? Almost five weeks, now. You kept them in the same school district so they could finish out the school year. And stored all their stuff in your basement

4

when Lila couldn't keep up the rent payments . . ."

Mrs. Kovacs was apologetic. "I hated to turn them out of the apartment, but she didn't know when she'd be able to go back to work and pay rent. And the kids couldn't have stayed there by themselves, anyway. So when Mr. Hamilton came along and wanted to rent the place, it seemed sensible to let him have it and move the kids here. I figured the Nortons would be moving out about the time Lila came home—or when I *thought* she was going to come home—and she could have that place. It's not quite as roomy, but it was the best I could think of."

"You've done wonders," Aunt Marge said. "Heaven knows *I* couldn't have taken the kids. Not three of them in a one-bedroom flat."

Rosie's chest was aching again as she strained to hear. She cast a quick glance at Kevin and saw that his face was grim, which frightened her.

Mrs. Kovacs had been their landlady for almost three years, and they liked her very much. Their mom and Mrs. Kovacs had become good friends, and the last time everyone else in the apartment house had their rent raised, the Gilberts' rent had remained the same because the landlady knew Lila Gilbert's pay hadn't gone up enough to cover an increase.

It was scary when their mother went into the hospital, Rosie remembered. It was the first time they'd ever been away from her overnight. But everybody had assured them that their mom would recover from the stroke and come home before long.

Rosie had always thought only old people got strokes. Even Mrs. Kovacs had thought that. But Aunt Marge said no, even young people could have strokes, especially if they'd had rheumatic fever when they were children, like Mama. Aunt Marge acted as if she'd known that all the time, but Rosie thought she'd found out after Mama got sick, the same as the rest of them had learned it.

"At least it wasn't as bad as it could have been," Aunt Marge had said. "Lila's probably going to be able to come home within a few weeks."

Now it seemed that it was going to be much longer. Months, Mrs. Kovacs had said. Was she saying that she couldn't keep three kids any longer? Rosie wondered if it was something they'd done; Mrs. Kovacs had scolded Nathan about keeping frogs in the bathtub, and Kevin was careless about picking up apple cores and putting them in the garbage. And she herself, Rosie thought anxiously, had forgotten to straighten up her closet the way Mrs. Kovacs had asked her to do. Was that why they couldn't stay here until Mama was well?

The blood thundered in her ears, and for a few moments Rosie didn't hear what was being said in the kitchen below. Then she caught sight of Kevin's face and breathed through her mouth, forcing the inside of her head to be quiet enough so she could pick up the conversation again.

"How can they do that?" Aunt Marge was demanding, sounding angry. "Nobody's even spoken to *me,* and I'm the one who should make the decision if Lila's too sick to do it."

What decision? Rosie wondered, not daring to ask Kevin what had been said while she was temporarily stricken deaf, for fear she'd miss what was being said *now.*

Nathan leaned into her side, and Rosie put an arm

around him instinctively. He'd gone and gotten his glasses, as if having them on would help him to hear better.

"I don't know," Mrs. Kovacs said. "They do all kinds of things these days, whether people want them to or not. But I'm only a landlady—an *ex*-landlady at that—and nobody's going to listen to what *I* say. I have to admit, I don't quite know how to manage with three kids if it's the end of the summer before Lila can come home, and they said it might be. I'm supposed to be going to stay with my sister in Florida, you know, when she has her operation next month. I couldn't take the kids with me, nor leave them here alone, either one. But the way that woman spoke, it didn't sound as if I'd have anything to say about it, anyway. She said it would be up to the social workers, and she thought they were planning to put the kids into foster homes."

"Homes?" Aunt Marge echoed, outraged. "Split them up, into more than one foster home?"

Rosie's stomach lurched, and she felt as if she were going to throw up. A shudder ran through her little brother, and she hugged him tighter, as much for her own comfort as for Nathan's.

"She said most foster parents don't want to take on more than one child at a time," Mrs. Kovacs said. "It's a shame, when their daddy died of that pneumonia, and now their mama's so sick, too, for them to lose each other, even for a few months."

"It's outrageous," Aunt Marge said. "If it wasn't for having to go off with Mr. Martinelli on business trips all the time—he has two of them coming up in the next ten days— maybe I could come stay here with the kids while you're in Florida. Only of course I could only be here nights and weekends. I can't take any time off from my job, except for two weeks of vacation, and that's not until late August. I can't think what to do!''

"Lila never talked about any family, except for you and the old aunt who went into a rest home," Mrs. Kovacs said. "Isn't there anybody else who could keep them for the summer? There's a chance Lila will be well enough to come home by the time school starts.''

There was a short silence, and then Aunt Marge said, "No, there's only Lila and me." She cleared her throat. "She had it arranged for Mrs. Critelli to look after the kids again through the summer, but she'd have to be paid her usual wage, and *I* certainly don't have the money to do that. There's no telling how long it will be before Lila's ready to work again, and *she* doesn't have any funds to pay a sitter.''

"What are we going to do, then?''

Aunt Marge spoke in a flat, harsh voice. "I don't know. I don't think you should say anything about this to the kids yet. They've been upset enough without having to worry about this, too.''

"That's what I thought," Mrs. Kovacs said.

"We haven't heard anything officially from the social services people," Aunt Marge continued. "This Ms. Hayboldt may be mistaken about them placing the kids in foster homes.''

Mrs. Kovacs' voice was so low that Rosie could barely make out her words. "She sounded like she knew what she was talking about. She said they'd be contacting me day after tomorrow. She said . . . she said Lila had already signed the papers.''

Rosie turned a stricken face to Kevin. "It can't be true, can it? Mama wouldn't just give us away!''

Kevin's whisper was fierce. "She's sick. She knows she can't take care of us. Maybe she's so sick they made her sign, even if she didn't want to."

Down below, there were sounds of cups and saucers being placed in the sink. Aunt Marge spoke from the kitchen doorway, and the trio on the landing above retreated before she could emerge into the hallway and discover them there, eavesdropping.

"Well, we'll have to try to figure out something," Aunt Marge said, but to Rosie it didn't sound as if she believed they *could.*

Kevin padded silently back into the bedroom he shared with Nathan, and by unspoken consent the other two followed him. It was a nice room, big and sunny in the daytime, though it was shadowy now with only the small lamp burning beside the bed. It was a room much like the one where Rosie had been sleeping since they'd come here nearly five weeks ago.

It wasn't home, but she'd felt safe in Mrs. Kovacs' house, Rosie thought. She'd had Kevin and Nathan in the same house, and she'd thought Mama would be coming home any day.

Kevin threw himself on the bed, bouncing a little, and faced them angrily.

"We're not going into any foster homes," he said, his voice cracking. "We're not! Jesse Cormier at school has been in four foster homes, and he says they're all terrible!"

Nathan shoved his glasses up more securely on his nose. "Jodie Mitchell is in a foster home. She likes it a lot better than her old home. Nobody beats her anymore."

"They're not going to split us up," Kevin insisted.

Rosie hoped desperately for a miracle. "What are we going to do, then?"

For a moment it seemed that Kevin would not reply, and then he did. "We're going to run away," he said.

2 THEY SAT ON KEVIN'S BED FOR A LONG time, talking, while Rosie's legs grew cramped and her head began to ache.

The idea of running away from home—if they could call this home when it belonged to Mrs. Kovacs and she wasn't even related to them—terrified her. Yet it was even more frightening to think of being separated from Kevin and Nathan and going into a foster home. Some foster homes were okay, she knew. But others, like the ones where Jesse Cormier had been, sounded dreadful.

Daddy had died, Mama was in the hospital where she might not get well for a very long time, and her brothers were the only family Rosie had. She didn't want to live anywhere apart from them. Yet grown-ups were the ones who decided such things. Was it true that Mama had signed a paper saying that they could be divided up and sent to different foster homes?

Nathan's gravelly voice was barely above a whisper. "When Mama gets better, we'll all live together again, won't we?"

Kevin's face was grim in the dim light of the softly shaded lamp. "What if she doesn't get better?"

A tight, painful knot formed in Rosie's chest, and she couldn't speak. Nathan swallowed audibly.

"You mean she's going to die? Like Daddy?"

There was despair and a fear to match Rosie's in the older boy's face.

"I don't know. Maybe. Why else would Mama let them put us in foster homes?"

Rosie fought the need to cry. "The doctor said Mama would get better."

"Sometimes"—Kevin gulped—"doctors are wrong. Anyway, even if she does get well, it'll be a long time. We can't just sit around and wait while they split us up. We've got to do something about it."

In the silence, they heard the front door close downstairs. Aunt Marge had left. Or no, Rosie thought, sitting up straighter, someone else had come in, for there was a male voice.

"Hank's here," she said, glad to be diverted, if only for a moment, from the awful discussion.

Mama used to joke about Hank, calling him Mrs. Kovacs' boyfriend. Their landlady always laughed at the idea, though Rosie had noticed that sometimes she blushed a little.

"Nobody's needing a gentleman friend at my age," she'd say. "Mr. Kovacs left me with this house, bought and paid for, and the apartments. I can get by. I don't need a man to support me, and I like being independent. I miss my own Ernie, heaven knows, but I've got used to cooking just for myself, not having to pick up after anybody else. And that Hank is a pure slob, he is!"

Nevertheless, Mrs. Kovacs always seemed glad to see Hank when he showed up. Though she said she made cookies for the kids, she usually let Hank eat half of them. And she was always in a good mood when he was there; the two of them would sit at the kitchen table and drink coffee and laugh a lot while they talked.

Once Rosie had heard Mama say, with a wistful look on her face, "Don't you get lonesome, Mrs. Kovacs?"

And the landlady had grown solemn, too, and nodded. "That I do, Lila. It's a fact. Having you and the kids living just across the street helps a lot, you know? It's almost as if I had grandchildren."

Mr. and Mrs. Kovacs had had a daughter once, a long time ago. She had died before she could get married and have any children. Lots of people died, Rosie knew, and they weren't all old people. Some were as young as Mama and the Kovacses' daughter.

She slid off the bed and went to open the door, so as to hear better. Sure enough, it was Hank. Even when he tried to speak quietly, his voice had a booming quality that practically rattled the windows, Mrs. Kovacs said. She was shushing him now.

"Wasn't that Lila's sister, just left here?" Hank asked, attempting to be quieter. "What's she doing out this time of night?"

"I called her. We've got a crisis coming up. Come on out in the kitchen and have what's left of the cake, and I'll tell you about it. Poor little tykes."

They moved away, and Rosie felt no urge to move out onto the stairs to try to hear better. Eavesdropping had already been painful enough for one night.

She retreated to the bedroom, closing the door so their

own voices wouldn't carry to the adults below. *Poor little tykes.* The phrase echoed in her mind, and she remembered when she'd heard Mrs. Kovacs say the same thing before.

When Daddy died, Rosie thought. Her throat hurt and it was hard to swallow. Did Mrs. Kovacs really mean that Mama was dying, too?

Nathan and Kevin had continued to talk while Rosie was at the doorway. Now Kevin included her in his statement: "We're going to have to run away if we want to stay together."

Nathan considered this gravely. "Where are we going to go?"

"I don't know yet, exactly. But we can't stay here or those social services people will come and get us and do what they want, without asking what *we* want."

Rosie thought of sleeping under trees or in abandoned barns. It might not be too bad now, in the summer, but what about when it got cold in the fall? And how would they eat?

"We don't have any money," she said softly.

"We can't steal any," Nathan murmured. "Mama wouldn't like that."

"I wish we knew how much time we have before they come to get us," Kevin said, as if to himself. "It might not be very long. We need to make plans as soon as we can, before it's too late."

"If only we had some relative besides Aunt Marge," Nathan said. "Only, like she said, there isn't anybody else. If Mama dies, we'll be orphans, won't we?"

Rosie suddenly remembered the way Aunt Marge had hesitated, for just a few seconds, when Mrs. Kovacs had asked about anyone else who could take the three of them for the summer. And then Aunt Marge had said in that odd tone, "No, there's only Lila and me."

Because that wasn't strictly true, and now Rosie spoke without thinking. "There's Grandmother," she said.

In the silence they heard the rumble of Hank's voice from downstairs, although they couldn't make out the words.

Kevin's mouth dropped open. "Yeah. That's it, Rosie! We'll go to Grandmother's house! She'll have to take us in, won't she? After all, we're her own daughter's children!"

Nathan shoved his glasses higher on the bridge of his nose. "But we don't even know her. Mama hasn't spoken to her since before any of us were born."

Already Rosie was sorry she'd put the idea into words. Already she was remembering that Mama and Aunt Marge always looked funny when there was any mention of Grandmother Woodruff, and they refused to talk about their mother except to say that they had been estranged for years. Estranged, Rosie had decided, was a polite way of saying they didn't talk to each other anymore.

Actually, from what Rosie understood, their grandmother had sent her two little girls away to live with their aunt Maude when they were very small. Rosie thought their mother had come to visit occasionally, at first, but then had stopped coming. They hadn't seen or heard from her in years. There hadn't even been a reply from her when Aunt Marge wrote to Grandmother to say that Aunt Maude had to go into a nursing home; Rosie remembered because she'd overheard Aunt Marge and her mother talking; they'd both been upset, and Mama had wiped her eyes furiously.

"No," Rosie said. "I don't know why I thought about her. Of course we can't go there. In fact, we don't even know where she lives."

"Probably still where she lived when Mama and Aunt Marge were little girls. In Missouri. That's not so far, just across the state line from Illinois." Kevin screwed up his face, concentrating. "I should be able to think of the town, if I try hard. Mama used to mention where she started school."

It had been a terrible idea, Rosie thought wildly. Why had she made such an awful suggestion? Of course they couldn't go to the grandmother who was hated by her own daughters! "If Mama had wanted us to go there," she said, "she'd have told somebody by this time. She wouldn't want us to do it!"

"Mama's sick," Kevin said, sounding hard. "Too sick to know what she's doing, or she'd never be turning us over to someone else. Maybe she even knows she's dying, and wants to make arrangements before it's too late." Tears shimmered in his blue eyes.

"Stop saying that!" Rosie protested through the ache in her throat. "Mrs. Kovacs said she might be well enough to come home by the time school starts! She *did,* Kevin, just a little while ago, to Aunt Marge!"

"Mrs. Kovacs is an optimist," her brother reminded her. "Remember, she said herself she kept expecting Mr. Kovacs to get better right up to the day he died. We can't wait and see what happens, Rosie. If they've already separated us, we may never be able to get back together again, don't you see? Listen, where are those old books of Mama's, and papers? There was a report card in it, from when she

16

was in kindergarten, remember? She showed it to us, to prove what a good student she was. And it would have the name of the school, and the town. The town where Grandmother lives."

"I don't want to go there," Rosie asserted. "I don't know why I said such a crazy thing."

It was as if Kevin didn't hear her. "I'm going to look for it first thing in the morning. I think the boxes are in the basement."

"I'm an optimist, too," Rosie stated. "I believe Mama's going to get well and come and get us."

"Well, that's what I hope happens, too," Kevin agreed, hugging his knees as he rocked back on the bed. "But there's the whole rest of the summer, and we've got to stay together. I read the other day about two old men who had just been reunited after seventy years; they were taken by different families to raise when they were only five and seven years old, and they'd been looking for each other ever since they grew up. I don't want that to happen to *us*, Rosie."

"I don't want it to happen, either," Nathan said. His eyes were very large behind his thick glasses.

Rosie said nothing, and Kevin nodded as if they were all three in agreement.

"We'll look for the report card tomorrow," he decreed. "And when we know where the town is, we'll run away to Grandmother's house."

He made it sound easy, but it wouldn't be easy, Rosie thought. She got up to return to her own room, knowing there was no point in arguing with her brothers any further tonight.

Maybe by morning she'd have thought of something that made more sense than going to a grandmother who probably wasn't even aware they existed and wouldn't want to know them anyway, since she'd given away her own daughters all those years ago.

Hank was just leaving as Rosie came out onto the landing. His "quiet" voice carried clearly to her.

"Don't seem right," he was saying to Mrs. Kovacs. "They hadn't ought to be able to parcel kids out like they was apples or something."

"Well, you argue with the social services people," Mrs. Kovacs snorted. "They mean well, I suppose, but some of 'em don't seem to have much common sense."

"Compassion, that's what they need. Compassion for homeless kids," Hank said.

A shiver ran through Rosie. Homeless kids. Was that them, her and Kevin and Nathan? Please, God, let her think of something to do!

"I'll see you tomorrow night," Hank told Mrs. Kovacs, opening the front door. "Drop in for a cup of coffee before I get on the road to Kansas City. Got another trailer to deliver just this side of there, and your grub's a lot tastier than what they cook up in that Fanny's Place. That's the only place open when I need to stop for breakfast on the way, early in the morning. I'll be back by the weekend. What do you say to a night out on Saturday, take in a movie and maybe even a dance?"

"I'm too old for dancing," Mrs. Kovacs said tartly. "And you forget, I've got three young ones here. I can't go off for hours and leave them alone."

Rosie didn't stay to hear the reply, stumbling into her

own room with tears stinging her eyes. They were a burden
even to Mrs. Kovacs. Maybe Kevin was right about running
away, though she desperately hoped they would be able to
think of somewhere to go other than to a mysterious and
frightening grandmother.

She slid into bed, and although she'd already said her
prayers earlier, she said them again. Twice couldn't hurt,
when they needed help so badly, she thought.

3 MRS. KOVACS ASKED NO QUESTIONS when they disappeared into the basement right after breakfast. In a way she was easier to live with than Mama, who always wanted to know what they were doing as well as where they were. Mrs. Kovacs took it for granted that they were behaving acceptably as long as they were in the house or yard and she didn't hear anything crashing or people screaming.

The things that had been moved from their apartment to be stored in Mrs. Kovacs' house were stacked in a corner. Kevin was the strongest, so he lifted each box down and Nathan and Rosie began to open them unless whatever was written on the side made it clear its contents wouldn't include old report cards.

After an hour they still hadn't found the right box, and they were getting dirty. It was amazing how fast the dust had settled over everything. Nathan announced that he was hungry, and Rosie was dispatched to the kitchen for provisions because she was the cleanest and would attract less attention if Mrs. Kovacs saw her.

The landlady was on the telephone, however, in the living room, and as Rosie helped herself to apples and graham crackers, she overheard a little of the conversation.

"Well, I beg your pardon, Ms. Hayboldt, but it doesn't sound reasonable to me." Mrs. Kovacs was indignant, and upon hearing the name, Rosie almost dropped the cracker box. Ms. Hayboldt was the social services lady. "No, today would not be convenient. And you can tell whatever her name is that she'd be wasting her time to show up here without legal papers saying she's got a right to take the children, because I won't turn them over to her otherwise."

Rosie's heart seemed to stop. Her fingernails punched through the wrapping on the box she carried, and she had to make an effort to breathe because her chest was paralyzed.

"Monday?" Mrs. Kovacs was saying. Her voice carried almost as well as Hank's did, because she was upset and had forgotten to control it. "Ten o'clock. She'll be here at ten o'clock on Monday. Very well, but you tell her what I said. If she doesn't have a court order—yes, I understand that. In the meantime, I've a mind to call my lawyer."

Rosie gulped, turned, and plunged down the cellar steps, almost falling on the last one.

"What's the matter?" Kevin asked, accepting one of the apples. "What's happened?"

When Rosie told him about the part of the conversation she'd overheard, he forgot to chew the bite of apple he'd just taken.

"Wow. That's even sooner than I expected. It means we have to find that report card even faster than I thought. Hey, that box says pictures! Didn't Mama keep other things

21

with those? Souvenirs, keepsakes, that kind of thing? Here," he said, opening up the carton, "you each take a stack of this stuff. I'll bet it's in this mess somewhere."

Ordinarily, Rosie would have enjoyed looking at the pictures as she sorted through them. There was one of them as a family, when Daddy was still alive, before Nathan wore glasses. Rosie put it on the discard stack and kept searching. They wouldn't even be *part* of a family for long, if they were put in separate foster homes.

A moment later, Nathan said, "Here it is! It says Sunnyside School."

"Where?" Kevin took the card and held it up to the light. "Missouri, like I said. Nettleford, Missouri!"

Rosie's mouth was so dry it was hard to speak. "It's from a long time ago, Kevin. Grandmother may not live there anymore."

"Of course she does. Why would she move?" Kevin asked. "She must be an old lady, older even than Mrs. Kovacs. Old ladies don't like to move. Now we have to figure out where Nettleford is and how to get there without any money. I know Mama always said it isn't safe to hitchhike, but—"

"No," Rosie said quickly. "Even with three of us, that's too dangerous. Let's get a map and find out where it is, how far away. Maybe we could walk. Even if it takes a few days . . . It's not cold out at night, and we've got sleeping bags. We could roll them up and strap them on our backs—"

"And pick things to eat from the fields and the orchards," Nathan added.

"Nothing's ripe yet," Kevin pointed out. "It's too early. I'm sure Mrs. Kovacs wouldn't mind if we made a bunch of sandwiches or something to carry with us. But I think it's too far to walk unless we take half the summer, and we can't carry enough food to last that long."

"In books, people do work at farms along the way, and the farmers' wives feed them," Nathan recalled.

"That might work," Kevin conceded. "Or maybe if we asked, they'd take pity on us because we're kids, and we're skinny, and they'd feed us without making us work much."

"Or more likely they'd call the police to see why we were wandering around the country alone," Rosie suggested. "Isn't that the stuff that came out of the glove compartment when we had to sell the car? See if there's a map of Missouri so we can tell how far we'd have to go."

She was afraid of running away to a grandmother they didn't know, but she was even more frightened of staying here at the mercy of strangers who would decide their fate. She reached into the jumble of odds and ends. "Here're the maps. One of Illinois, one of Arkansas, and one of Missouri."

They spread the last one out on top of the boxes, and Kevin ran a finger over it. "There's nearly enough of Illinois on the edge to show where we are now. Off here." He tapped a spot on top of the box. "Now where's Nettleford?"

They found it listed under *Cities and Villages,* and Kevin decided it could only be classified as a village. "Six hundred and forty people," he observed with mounting satisfaction. "In a town that size, it shouldn't be hard to find Grandmother. It's in *D* going down and *2* across."

Using a finger on each hand, he tracked it down. To Rosie it looked impossibly far from the Illinois border, way closer to the western edge of the state than to their own side of it.

Disappointment swept over her. "We couldn't walk it. Not in weeks."

"Not without getting caught. Or starving while we were doing it," Kevin agreed. "It's practically to Kansas City."

"How many miles is it?" Nathan asked, also peering at the map, but Rosie interrupted him.

"Hank's going to Kansas City again. Just this side of it, anyway. Tonight."

Kevin sat back on his heels and wiped sweat off his forehead, leaving a dirty smear. "To deliver a trailer? Are you sure?"

"I heard him say so. He's coming to have coffee with Mrs. Kovacs before he goes." Was this the answer to her prayer? Rosie wondered. "He always waits until rush hour is over before he leaves. If it's almost to Kansas City, which way would he go? Would he get very near to Nettleford, do you think? Close enough so maybe we *could* walk the rest of the way?"

Kevin studied the map again. "Well, he might go on Highway 136, here." His finger traced the red line across the top of the map, turning when the highway intersected with Interstate 35 to run down to Kansas City. "That would take us practically to Grandmother's front door. Or he could start south as soon as he crosses the Mississippi and drive down until he gets to here. Highway 36. That would be maybe"—he calculated in his head—"probably thirty miles from Nettleford, if he went that way. I guess we could walk thirty miles, though it might take us a couple of days."

Rosie stared at the map. Below the highways he had

indicated was a heavier red line. "What if he goes all the way down here, to Interstate 70? That's a freeway, and it would be faster driving, wouldn't it? But that would bring us way down here. A lot farther away from Grandmother's house."

If only Hank had said exactly where he was going! But then, he usually didn't, because it was mostly to farms outside of cities. Hank's brother-in-law owned a small company that made horse trailers, and Hank had a job delivering them. Only last week he'd taken one to Kentucky, and once he'd gone to Tennessee. Mostly he delivered them near Kansas City or St. Louis. He liked to drive at night, especially in the summer, because it was cooler then, and also there was less traffic.

Kevin reevaluated the route. "I don't think he'll go down to I-70," he said finally. "It's the best road, but to get to it he'd have to either follow the river too far back to the east or cut across on those secondary roads. He doesn't like to get on narrow roads, and those black lines mean they're not very good roads. I'd bet on either of the top ones, here. Either way, we ought to get close to Nettleford. A lot closer than we are now."

"Close enough to walk," Nathan said in his froggy tones.

Rosie stared at her older brother. "So are we going to try it?"

Kevin's hesitation was brief. "Let's do it," he said. "Get a pencil, Rosie, and make a list of what we need to do before Hank gets here tonight with the trailer. There'll be a whole bunch of stuff to take, and take care of."

"And we can't make Mrs. Kovacs suspicious," Rosie cautioned.

Her heart was pounding again as she held the stub of pencil over a piece of paper she'd torn from a note pad in the box where they'd found the maps.

"Food," she wrote, and waited for Kevin and Nathan to come up with the rest.

4 HANK WAS SO LATE THAT THEY'D begun to think he wouldn't come.

"Maybe somebody canceled the order for the horse trailer," Nathan guessed, adjusting his glasses.

"Or Hank's running late so he didn't stop here for coffee after all," Kevin said.

"He'll be here," Rosie said doggedly, hoping she was right. Hank *had* to come, or they had no way to get to Nettleford, where their grandmother lived. All day she had worried, and now she blurted, "What if Grandmother doesn't want us any more than she wanted Mama and Aunt Marge? What'll we do then?"

Kevin gave her one of his looks of blended irony and wry amusement. "The same thing we'll do if we stay here and don't try, I guess: Let the social services people decide what happens to us."

"I thought those people were supposed to help kids in trouble," Nathan said.

"They do, sometimes." They were in Rosie's bedroom

because it was the one with the window overlooking the alley; that was where Hank always parked the horse trailers when he stopped for a brief visit before going off. It was a good thing the trailer would be in the back of the house; they'd have had difficulty in loading it if it were out front where the neighbors could see it. "I suppose they try to pick good foster homes for kids, only they don't always know how it's going to work out. But no matter how good the homes might be, we're not going to three different ones, not if we can help it." Kevin wandered to the window and looked out, for the tenth time in the last quarter of an hour. "Where is he? Are you sure he said tonight, Rosie?"

"Yes," Rosie replied quietly, but her nerves were screaming with the need to *do* something.

It hadn't been so bad during the day while they were still making their list, then checking each item off as it was gathered up. The boys had managed to haul almost everything out behind the garage off the alley while Rosie made sure Mrs. Kovacs wasn't in the rear of the house where she could see them.

"I hope it's a big trailer this time," Kevin said, letting the curtains fall back into place. "Then we can take sleeping bags, too, and be comfortable."

"And the suitcases," Rosie added. She hated to leave all her clothes. Grandmother might not want to buy them new ones.

"I told you," Kevin warned, not leaving the window, "that if we have to walk very far, we're going to have to abandon the heaviest stuff. We can't walk thirty miles or more carrying everything we've got out there."

"I'm hungry," Nathan put in. "Did we leave out anything to eat?"

"No, it's all in bags, behind the garage. Hey! Look, here he comes! It's Hank, all right, and he's got a really big trailer! I think it's one of those with a sleeper in the front, so we'll even have beds!" Kevin's face lit up in excitement.

Rosie didn't know if she felt excited or scared, only that her stomach was queasy. In fact, as she stood beside her brothers watching what they could see of the shiny new burgundy horse trailer behind Hank's pickup, she wondered if she were going to throw up.

"Come on," Kevin said. "Let's go down and see if we can get in on the cake when she cuts it for Hank, and then Rosie can divert their attention again while we load the trailer."

Rosie stood frozen at the window when the boys moved away. "What if he looks in the trailer and sees our stuff?"

"Why would he do that? He never carries anything in the trailers. He just puts the toolbox and that little overnight bag with a change of clothes in the back of his truck. The trailer will be empty, and he won't check it except on the outside. You know, tires and stuff. Come on."

Rosie hesitated on the landing, wondering if she needed to use the bathroom before she went downstairs. Until now, that hadn't occurred to her: How were they going to ride for hours in the horse trailer without a bathroom?

She let her brothers go on ahead, then stared at her face in the bathroom mirror after she'd washed her hands. Would Mrs. Kovacs know by looking at her that something was up?

Apparently not. Their benefactor was serving cake, which oddly enough was called Boston cream pie, when Rosie entered the kitchen. She was handed a plate with a slice of it: tender yellow cake with a cream filling between the layers and a rich chocolate frosting on the outside.

"Melts in your mouth," Hank said, grinning, as he stuck his fork in for a second bite. "Fortifies a man for a long run, darned if it don't."

"You going far this time?" Kevin asked casually, licking chocolate off his thumb.

"Brayfill Farms. North of K.C. about seventy miles." Hank lifted his coffee cup toward Mrs. Kovacs. "You got another cup of that brew, ma'am? Won't get any more this good until I come back. They got pretty waitresses and pretty fair pie in that Fanny's Place, but they can't match your coffee, Mrs. K."

Kevin shot Rosie a sly, satisfied grin. Seventy miles north of Kansas City, he was saying without words, would take them right through Nettleford. They wouldn't have to walk thirty miles.

Mrs. Kovacs passed back the steaming cup. "Fine way to talk to somebody that's feeding you her own mother's recipe for Boston cream pie, not to mention the coffee. Pretty waitresses, is it?"

Hank grinned. "Aw, they're all too young for an old goat like me. Besides, Fanny's is the only place open on the Interstate so early in the morning. Folks around Daviess County are mostly farmers, and they don't get their morning chow in restaurants, so it's mainly truckers that stop there."

Mrs. Kovacs snorted. "Pretty waitresses," she muttered, not quite forgiving him yet. "Well, it's getting late. You kids better be off to bed pretty soon. Especially you, Nathan. You're looking worn out. You're not getting sick, are you?"

"No," Nathan said, in his usual slow way. "Rosie's going

to read me a story before I get ready for bed."

"And then I'm going to take my new library book and read in bed to myself," Rosie said, the way she'd rehearsed. "I'll say good-night when we go up."

Kevin sounded almost suspiciously casual, Rosie thought with some anxiety, when he added, "Me, too. I got a new mystery book by Bill Wallace. His are always good. I'll probably read the whole thing, so don't worry if I sleep in tomorrow morning."

He was overdoing it, Rosie thought, trying to give him a quelling look, but he wasn't paying any attention to her. And neither Hank nor Mrs. Kovacs seemed to notice anything.

"I've got to go out early tomorrow," Mrs. Kovacs said, settling at the table with her own slice of cake. "It's our day to set up the rummage sale at church. I'll probably be there most all day; I reckon you three can shift for yourselves for breakfast and lunch, can't you?"

"Oh, sure," Kevin said. "Don't worry about us." He gave Rosie another smug look, and she kicked him under the table. If he wasn't careful, Mrs. Kovacs would *know* something was up.

The boys said their good-nights, but Rosie cleared her throat and asked if it was all right if she had a glass of milk. She heard the boys going upstairs, but though she knew they had immediately sneaked silently back down, she couldn't hear them. Presumably that meant Mrs. Kovacs and Hank hadn't heard them either as they slipped out the front door and would now be circling the house.

Hank patted his stomach and pushed back his chair after only a few minutes. "Well, that was delicious. The only kind of cake I like better is your German chocolate. I better get on the road. I got an all-night drive ahead of me."

Rosie nearly panicked. It was too soon for him to go. The boys might not have loaded everything yet, and *she* still had to get into the trailer unseen as well.

Rosie's mind skittered around frantically, searching for something to delay him briefly. "Uh . . . Mrs. Kovacs, wasn't there something you wanted Hank to do while he was here?"

Mrs. Kovacs looked blank. "Was there?"

"Uh . . . in the basement? Something for the rummage sale, maybe? Weren't you going to get down those tools of Mr. Kovacs', up on the high shelves?"

"Did I say that? I don't remember. But it's a good idea. And they are sort of heavy to lift from so high up. Would you have time, Hank? I don't want to make you late."

"Ah, won't take but a few minutes to do that," Hank said easily. "Sure thing."

Rosie drained her glass of milk so quickly she nearly choked on it. "Well, good-night, everybody."

"Good-night, good-night." They were moving toward the cellar door and the tools for the rummage sale, and Rosie fairly flew out the back door.

It wasn't quite dark yet, though it wasn't really light, either. She tripped going down the back steps and went sprawling, feeling the sting of scraped skin on one elbow, then was up and running.

"He coming?" Kevin hissed as she rounded the garage.

"In the basement," Rosie gasped. "He'll be here in a minute. Hurry!"

"Nathan's already in the trailer. All we have to do is get

in ourselves," Kevin assured her. "Come on, quick."

He swung the front side door of the horse trailer open and practically boosted her in ahead of him. It was dark inside the forward compartment, or at least it seemed so until her eyes adjusted. She stumbled over something on the floor, then felt the edge of one of the bunks where the handlers would sleep when they were moving horses around.

There was no horse smell, of course. There hadn't been any horses in the trailer yet. All she could smell was peanut butter. Rosie collapsed onto the bunk and heard Nathan's froggy tones from overhead.

"You want a sandwich?"

"On top of two pieces of cake you're eating a sandwich? No, thanks," Rosie managed, and lay still, catching her breath.

There was a soft *snick* as Kevin latched the door behind him. "Boy, that was kind of close. He's coming now," he said, easing onto the bunk beside Rosie. "Hey, what a break, huh? Mrs. Kovacs will be going out early, so she won't miss us until suppertime tomorrow. We'll be there, by then. She won't know where we are so she won't be able to tell that Ms. Hayboldt where we went, even if she wants to. She doesn't even know we have a grandmother. We'll have to keep everything clean in here, so nobody suspects this is how we left."

"The smell of peanut butter will give us away," Rosie muttered, and then fell silent as she heard Mrs. Kovacs call out, "Good-bye, Hank."

"See you this weekend," Hank called back. "Maybe you can get a sitter so we can go out Saturday night after all."

33

"I'm too old for that nonsense," Mrs. Kovacs replied, though Rosie thought she sounded pleased.

And then, as guilt washed over her and she held her breath, praying that Hank wouldn't look into the trailer and find them, Rosie wondered if Mrs. Kovacs would feel like taking in a movie or a dance after she'd discovered they were missing.

Rosie had insisted upon writing a note, which was on her pillow, for when their landlady discovered that they were gone, that the shapes in their beds were only pillows or rolled blankets. They couldn't let Mrs. Kovacs believe they'd been kidnapped or some such horrid thing; they had to tell her they were leaving because they didn't want to be sent to separate foster homes. They were undoubtedly a nuisance to her, but Rosie thought she'd be concerned about them. She'd been very good to them since all the trouble had begun with their mother's illness.

The door of the pickup slammed, and the motor purred to life. A moment later, they were under way.

Kevin sighed in relief. "It's going to work," he said. "To Grandmother's house we go!"

Rosie rolled over. "You're sitting on me. How many bunks are there?"

"Only two. I'll spread my sleeping bag on the floor. I already tried it. It's not bad. I could move back into the horse stalls and have more room, but I'll just curl up a little. I figure we have about two hundred and forty miles to go, maybe two hundred and fifty. Say Hank averages fifty miles an hour—he drives legal, at fifty-five, but he'll stop a couple of times, probably, so figure fifty miles an hour—that means we ought to be passing near Nettleford in about five hours. Maybe six if he stops to eat again tonight. It's about nine-thirty now, isn't it? Quarter to ten? So we'll be there be-tween three and four o'clock in the morning."

"It'll still be dark," Rosie said. It wasn't cold, but she shivered.

"All the better," Kevin told her, moving off the bunk to settle onto his sleeping bag on the floor. "Nobody'll notice us getting out."

"How are we going to make Hank stop near Nettle-ford?" Nathan asked suddenly in the darkness.

There was a moment of silence before Kevin spoke. "I don't know. We'll have to figure out something. Anyway, I looked on the map. Hank said Daviess County is where that Fanny's Place is. And Nettleford's in Daviess County, too. So if we're lucky we won't be too far off base."

"How are we going to know when it's time to get out?" Rosie asked. "How'll we know where we are?"

"I brought the map and a flashlight, and we can watch out for road signs," Kevin explained, though he seemed less certain than he had earlier that all of this would work out satisfactorily. "Right now, though, we'd better get some sleep."

"What if we sleep past Nettleford?" Nathan persisted.

"We won't. Besides, he isn't going all that far past, if it's the distance he said north of Kansas City. We said we could walk thirty miles over a couple of days if we had to, remember?"

"But if we don't wake up before he reaches the ranch, somebody may see us getting out," Rosie pointed out.

"At three or four in the morning? No way. They won't be up. Hank always plans to get there in time to get a few hours' sleep before he heads back."

"What if he decides to sleep back here in the bunks?"

Rosie didn't want to throw obstacles in the way of Kevin's theories about how easy this was going to be, but she couldn't help thinking of things that could go wrong. "Why would he sleep in the pickup when it would be more comfortable back here?"

"He always sleeps in the truck," Kevin said patiently. "If he intended to sleep in the trailer, he'd have brought a sleeping bag, like we did. He didn't put a thing back here. I once heard him tell Mrs. Kovacs he learned to sleep in the cab of a truck when he drove long-line, in the days before cabs had sleepers, and he doesn't mind it that much. Come on, let's get some sleep. I'll wake up and keep track of where we are. Don't worry."

Rosie lay on her back looking up into blackness. *Don't worry,* her mind echoed. *Easier said than done,* she thought.

5

ROSIE SLEPT DREAMLESSLY UNTIL SHE heard the boys' voices.

"Where are we?" Nathan demanded, and Kevin replied, "We crossed the Mississippi at Keokuk, and now we're getting close to Princeton; I just saw the sign. Hank's going the way I thought he would, all right."

Rosie couldn't remember where Princeton was on the map. "Is it time to wake up?"

"No. Go back to sleep," Kevin said, and Rosie slid gratefully into a dream about a smiling, rosy-faced grandmother who looked like Mrs. Kovacs, greeting them with a plate of gingerbread.

The next thing she knew, Kevin's hand was on her shoulder, shaking her. "Hank hasn't stopped at all so far, except to gas up once and use a rest room, so he's bound to stop at Fanny's Place, like he said. We just crossed the Daviess County line, so it can't be much farther."

Rosie came wide awake. She didn't have any difficulty in recalling that if they overshot the right place, they might have a long hike ahead of them.

She swung her legs over the edge of the bunk and sat up, groping in the dimness for her shoes. It was cool enough so she was glad she had brought a sweater; she shrugged into it and rolled up her sleeping bag, though if Hank didn't stop, there would be no way to unload either their belongings or themselves.

As if he'd read her thoughts, Kevin said, "We'll have to get every single thing of ours out of here, or they'll figure out we stowed away with Hank. Aunt Marge might realize where we are, and they'll come after us. After all, she knows about Grandmother Woodruff, even if nobody else does."

Rosie was still shivering in spite of the sweater. "I wish we knew what happened between Mama and Aunt Marge and Grandmother."

"They probably had a big fight about something," Kevin said, sounding muffled as he knelt over his own sleeping bag, "and they just never made up."

Rosie was barely tall enough to see out the side windows when she stood up. Not that there was much of anything to see: shadowy trees and open fields, with an occasional farmhouse and outbuildings still dark in the predawn. It was all strange and unsettling.

"Grown-ups don't have fights and stay mad for years," she said softly. "At least . . . it would have to be a very serious fight . . . about something important."

Nathan was squirming around in the top bunk. His voice was froggier than ever when he first woke up. "It was Grandmother who gave them away, wasn't it? To Aunt Maude. When they were only little. How could a grown-up have a fight with kids and give them away like they were puppies or something?"

Rosie stared out onto the deep gray landscape. Far across a cornfield was a bobbing light. A farmer, going out to round up his cows for milking? She didn't know much about farms, but Mama had once mentioned living on a farm before Grandmother gave her away to Aunt Maude, and had said her father had gotten up when it was still dark to milk cows.

Rosie seemed to remember that Grandpa Woodruff had died when he was young, like Daddy, in some kind of farm accident. Apparently Mama and Aunt Marge didn't remember him very well, though once in a while they'd mentioned him. He had taken them to the county fair and let them ride the Ferris wheel and the merry-go-round, though he had refused to allow the roller coaster ride they had longed for. "Next year, he said," Rosie remembered Mama saying when she told the story. "Only there wasn't any next year. A month or so later he died, and the next spring we went to Aunt Maude's. And we never went to another county fair."

Bad things happened to a lot of people, Rosie thought with a lump in her throat. You never knew what was going to happen to you next, and if you were a kid there wasn't much you could do about anything.

Except, maybe, to run away when one of the bad things was coming at you. Yet for all she knew, the running away could be one of the bad things itself.

Kevin stood up and swung his sleeping bag onto the bunk beside Rosie's. "Anybody have a bright idea about how to make Hank stop when we see the sign for Nettleford if this Fanny's Place isn't until we go past it? Nettleford's not on the main highway; we'll still have to walk from wherever he stops. I can't believe he's not starving by now, though. He'll probably stop at Fanny's, all right."

"He had three pieces of the Boston cream pie last night," Rosie reminded him. "And a lot of coffee."

"Then you'd think he'd have to stop more often at a bathroom." Kevin scowled.

It was more fun reading about someone else's adventure than it was having one of your own, Rosie decided.

Nathan hit the floor with a thump when he slid off the top bunk. "If we dropped the peanut butter jar out the front window," he said, gesturing, "maybe it would cut a tire, and Hank'd have to stop."

"No," Rosie said quickly, before Kevin could reply, "we can't ruin a tire. They're awfully expensive, and Hank might have to pay for it. Besides, if he stops because of a flat tire, he's going to come back to the trailer to fix it. How are we going to get all this stuff out of there without him seeing it? And us?"

The houses were getting closer together, Rosie saw, which probably meant they were nearing a town. They had to think of something quick or they'd soon be getting farther away from Nettleford and Grandmother's house.

"Maybe we could make Hank *think* there's something wrong with a tire," Nathan said. "When we get to the edge of town, we could throw something that would make a racket, and he'd stop to investigate. Then, if there's a place to eat nearby, maybe he'd think about being hungry. It's been a long time since he had the cake. *I'm* hungry again."

Kevin bit his lip, then looked around. "What do we have that's heavy enough to make a noise if we pitch it into the back of his pickup? It's not a really good idea, Nate, but it's better than nothing."

Only they couldn't think of anything to throw that would make enough noise to alarm Hank. They stared at each other in growing panic, until suddenly Kevin stiffened. Rosie thought at first that something more was wrong, and then she caught it, too, the change in motion.

They were slowing down. Not to stop, Rosie decided, but because they were entering a town where there was a speed limit. And then, miracle of miracles, she saw that Hank *was* stopping. There was blinking red neon ahead, a restaurant open at this hour, and Hank was pulling in. Fanny's Place.

The trailer took up a lot of space, so he swung through the front parking lot and braked to a stop alongside a big refrigerator truck. A moment later, they heard the door slam, and Hank strode toward the lighted building.

"Now!" Kevin breathed, and opened the side door, shoving out sleeping bags and backpacks and the two suitcases.

When they jumped down beside the stack of stuff a few minutes later, Rosie stared at it in dismay.

"We're never going to be able to carry all this," she said, wondering if the tightness in her chest meant she was about to have a heart attack. Did ten-year-olds ever have heart attacks?

"No, we're not," Kevin confirmed. "But we can't leave it where it'll be found, at least not soon enough to be connected with Hank's horse trailer. Come on, hurry, help me drag the sleeping bags over behind that dumpster. Maybe nobody'll find them there for a while. I think we can carry the rest of it."

Rosie wasn't sure about that, but she followed Kevin's lead. It seemed a shame to leave the sleeping bags—they were good ones, and they'd probably never be able to afford any more—but even after they'd discarded them, it was all they could do to pick up the rest of their gear.

"Okay," Kevin said, after kneeling in the shelter of the dumpster to consult the map while he shielded the flashlight from anyone looking out the restaurant windows, "we're going to have to go farther into town and turn east when we get to the other highway. Three miles down that way is Nettleford."

Rosie looked back, just once. Hank was eating breakfast and talking to the other truck driver. He looked familiar and safe, and for a moment she wavered about going back to him and confessing what they'd done. Maybe they'd be better off letting Mrs. Kovacs and Aunt Marge do the best they could for them with the social services people.

And then the moment passed, because they'd already talked through all of that, and Mrs. Kovacs wasn't a relative, didn't owe them anything, and Aunt Marge couldn't take them, and Mama had signed some kind of papers. . . .

Eyes stinging, Rosie turned and trotted after her brothers.

They walked to the edge of the town and then into it.

A slow-moving police car drove them off the sidewalk into a darkened area between two houses where they crouched, holding their breaths, until it had passed. Another time a dog rushed at them, barking, and they ran until they were winded, which didn't take very long because of the backpacks and the suitcases.

What if Kevin had made a mistake? Rosie wondered as they slogged along after the dog had fallen back. What if this wasn't the town where they should have left the trailer? What if Grandmother didn't live in the same place anymore?

What if, she thought suddenly and uneasily, Grandmother, too, had died? Mama and Aunt Marge might not even have learned about it, if that were so.

Her legs felt wobbly from running with a heavy suitcase, and the tears were not far from the surface.

"Here's the cross highway," Kevin said. He was walking confidently, apparently without any worries about finding Grandmother or their reception when they reached her. He even grinned when he turned to speak to them.

At least they were headed right, then. Rosie could only hope his optimism would be justified when they reached the end of their journey.

There were a few cars now, people up early to go to work. Nobody stopped, though, or paid them any attention.

They walked and walked and walked. And finally they came to a small sign that said NETTLEFORD—POPULATION 640.

Kevin paused to rest the suitcase on the ground. "See? Nothing to it."

"We still have to find Grandmother's house," Nathan said. He hadn't spoken all the way from the other small town.

"She's probably in the phone book, and there's a phone booth in that gas station right over there. You guys wait here, and I'll go look," Kevin told them.

Rosie was glad to rest. She sat on the edge of the curb, and Nathan plopped down beside her.

"What if Grandmother doesn't want us?" he said gruffly.

It was exactly what she'd been worrying about herself, but when Nathan put it into words, Rosie was automatically encouraging. "It'll be okay. She's our grandmother, after all. Everybody knows grandmothers like kids."

Nathan just stared at her, owl-like, through his thick glasses. She had a feeling she hadn't cheered him up very much.

Kevin came back, grinning again. "There's only one Woodruff listed in the whole place, so it has to be her. It's on Woodruff Road, even. She's been here so long the road was named after her family."

"So where's Woodruff Road?" Rosie asked. The queasy feeling was back.

"I don't know, but this is such a little town we probably only have to walk through it and look at the street signs, and we'll see it."

"I'm hungry," Nathan said.

"Well, let's eat, then. There's a little park right up that way. A roadside rest area or something. There's a picnic bench. We can use the rest room, anyway, and then we'll find Woodruff Road."

They ate from the supplies in their backpacks: peanut butter and jelly sandwiches and apples, washed down with grape juice from paper cartons. They hadn't been able to bring much more than that, and Rosie hoped Grandmother would greet them with food by lunchtime.

They walked all the way through the village of Nettleford without finding Woodruff Road. Nobody here was up and around yet except for one old man opening up a store on the main street; he didn't seem to notice them, and they didn't want to call attention to themselves by asking directions of him. If anyone came looking for them here, he'd be sure to remember and say where they'd been going.

"What do we do now?" Rosie asked, staring up at the last of the street signs on the edge of town.

Kevin was beginning to look a bit weary, too. "Well, we didn't see it in town. That stands to reason, doesn't it? I mean, Grandmother lived on a farm when Mama was little, so it's probably out in the country a ways."

"How far?" Nathan demanded. "I'm tired."

"Probably not far," Kevin responded, and Rosie wondered if he, too, was just trying to make Nathan feel better. "Come on, we'll keep going along the main road and we'll probably come to it in a few minutes."

It was, in fact, half an hour. They kept walking because they didn't know what else to do, and the country seemed safer than the town, where someone was certain to wonder what three kids with all that baggage were doing by themselves.

At last Kevin gave a crow of delight. "There it is! Woodruff Road! See, I told you!"

It was not a painted metal sign, like the ones in the village, but a homemade one, with fading black letters on peeling white paint. Somehow, it made Rosie's uneasiness increase. It had an abandoned look.

That was how she was feeling. Abandoned. She reminded herself that she and Kevin and Nathan were still together, and that counted for something.

This time it was she who said, "Come on. Let's go."

There was another sign, just off the main road, one of the yellow ones with black letters that the county puts up. It said DEAD END.

None of them remarked on it, and they kept walking.

This road was gravel, not paved, and twenty minutes later, when Rosie had begun to think her legs weren't going to hold her up much longer—and her arms ached from carrying the suitcase—they saw it.

It was the right house, set well back from the road, because there was the name on the mailbox.

Rosie swallowed as a sickish feeling swept through her.

"I don't think this was such a good idea," she said weakly.

For once Kevin wasn't grinning.

He didn't say anything. Only Nathan spoke.

"It looks haunted," he said.

6

KEVIN MOISTENED HIS LIPS, LOOKING nervous. "Maybe we've got the wrong place," he said uncertainly.

Rosie sounded almost as froggy as Nathan. "It says Woodruff on the mailbox."

The sun was up now, but very little sunshine filtered through the trees and bushes ahead of them. The sycamores and spruce trees were huge and old, creating dense shade all around the house except for one small spot of color where a red bud flamed.

"Spooky," Nathan whispered, but Rosie knew he wasn't talking about the shadowy yard. He was talking about the house itself.

Rosie felt mesmerized by it. The few times that her mother and Aunt Marge had talked about the place where they'd been born and lived until after their father died, Rosie had pictured it as sunny and pleasant.

This was almost . . . sinister. The word crept into Rosie's mind, unwanted, chilling.

On the roof a TV antenna sagged sideways, as if it might

fall off entirely at any minute. The house was very big, of faded brick more nearly pink than red. There were two stories and an attic and many windows, most of them without curtains or shades. They reminded Rosie of the empty sockets in a skull Petie Padilla had brought to school once for show and tell.

Nathan was right. It *did* look haunted. Or at least abandoned.

"I don't think anybody lives here anymore," Rosie said, and was ashamed that her voice quavered. The queasiness was back. They'd come all this way for nothing, and they had no way to return home. No money. She felt like crying.

"It's . . . neglected," Kevin said, in a masterful understatement. "But maybe Grandmother's old and she can't do yard work anymore."

Rosie stared at the house. "Or do housework, or anything. What are we going to do now?"

Kevin tried to pull himself together; it was clear that he was as shaken as she was. "Well, we're here. If Grandmother's gone, we might as well look around our ancestral home and see if there's anything left that's useful."

"Useful for what?" Nathan wanted to know, echoing Rosie's unspoken thought. "We can't stay here by ourselves, can we?"

Kevin perked up a little. "We might. For a while, anyway."

"How would we eat?" Rosie asked bluntly. "We have enough left for a snack, not a full meal."

"There used to be an orchard, didn't there?" Kevin started up the driveway, and they fell into step beside him.

"What's ripe this early?" Rosie wanted to know. "If you

eat fruit too early, it gives you a bellyache. There might be berries, though." She brightened a little. "Some berries are ripe this time of year."

The empty "eyes" of the house, too high to peek into, seemed to follow them as they approached, following the dirt drive. The grass was deep on each side of it.

"Look," Nathan croaked suddenly, and they all stopped and followed his pointing finger.

There were windows here, too, on the back of the house; there was a sort of veranda across the rear of the building, between two projecting wings, and there was a trio of rocking chairs on the porch. But it was the windows in the nearer wing that Nathan was indicating.

"They had a fire," Kevin said slowly, gazing upward. "A long time ago, I think."

There were black marks on the faded brick where flames had spurted out the windows, which were still without glass except for a few broken shards in one frame.

Rosie's dream of a grandmother with a plate of gingerbread was fading. It wasn't so long ago that they'd had breakfast, but her stomach felt hollow already. They weren't going to have any luck getting a nice hot meal here, she thought.

"Hey," Nathan said, losing interest in the house, "back there, on the other side of the trees, I see something red. Isn't it berries?"

It was. Raspberries appeared in tangled, unpruned confusion when the children emerged from the thick woods around the house into what had once been a cleared area and a garden. Nathan started picking ripe berries, eating as he picked. "Mmm. They're good. Try some."

They all picked and ate for several minutes in silence. Rosie studied the garden, or what was left of it. Certainly nobody had hoed or weeded here in a long time, but there were a few ragged remnants of vegetables that had perhaps come up from last year's leavings. A tiny niggle of hope worked up through her chest. There might be enough for a few meals, anyway. That would give them time to make some kind of plans.

"There's the orchard, over there," Kevin said, swinging an arm beyond the open space that had once been a large garden area. "You're right, though, Rosie. Nothing ripe there yet. I wonder where that goes?"

"That" was an almost hidden path, long overgrown, but one that had once been graveled so that it was still discernible. It led past the end of the garden and off into the sycamores and spruces.

"Let's see where it goes," Nathan said eagerly, putting down his backpack. "It might be something interesting."

"Sure." Kevin was recovering a little from the shock of seeing Grandmother's house this way. He had already deposited the things he'd been carrying at the end of the row of raspberry bushes, and he grinned. "It probably goes to an outhouse."

Rosie stayed long enough to gather another handful of berries, then hurried along after her brothers. The underbrush pressed in on both sides of the path, scratching her arms as she passed, and the trees closed together overhead so that she felt almost as if she were swimming underwater in the greenish gloom.

Nathan came to such an abrupt halt ahead of her that Rosie stepped on his heels.

"What's the matter?" she asked, peering over his shoulder.

"There's a gate," Kevin said unnecessarily, for she could see it now, too.

It was wrought iron, and rusty. It hadn't been opened for years, from the look of it.

"Is it locked?" Nathan asked.

"No, but it's kind of rusted shut. Wait a minute, I think I can work it loose—ah!" Kevin gave a triumphant grunt and swung the gate open; its long-unused hinges protested loudly.

"What did they build a fence and a gate for, way out here in the woods?" Nathan wanted to know, but before anyone could hazard a guess, they all knew.

Hidden in the shadows, disguised by moss and undergrowth, it was unmistakably a small graveyard they had entered.

There were no more than a dozen or so headstones. Of her mother's family, Rosie realized. The Woodruffs who had been her ancestors were buried here.

It wasn't frightening in the graveyard; Rosie felt no chills up and down her spine the way she had when inspecting the house for the first time. Mostly she felt interest and curiosity.

They had known Daddy's family, what there was of it. Grandpa and Grandma Gilbert had died after Daddy had, Grandpa of a heart attack and Grandma of pneumonia only a short time later. Daddy only had one sister, and she'd married an Englishman and moved to Paris where her husband worked for a newspaper. Rosie's own family hadn't heard from that part of the family in over a year; Mama's last letter had been returned with a stamp saying that Aunt Evelyn and Uncle Roger had left no forwarding address.

Of the Woodruffs, however, Rosie knew very little. They saw Aunt Marge, of course, and once in a while they visited old Aunt Maude in the nursing home. Other than that, the Woodruff relatives were pretty much a mystery.

She bent over to peer at the nearest headstone, but it was so encrusted with moss and dirt she couldn't make out what it said. She reached for a stick and began to clean it off, then read aloud: "Albert Richard Woodruff. That's Grandpa Woodruff, Mama's father."

It gave her a funny feeling. Her own grandfather, whom she'd never known, lay beneath this headstone.

"Maybe," she said tentatively, "Grandmother's buried here, too."

"If she is," Kevin said, attacking the next headstone with a stick of his own, "it happened a long while ago. Nobody's been on that path recently."

"Let's find out," Rosie suggested. "You start over there, Nathan, and clean off the stones so we can read what they say. I'll take this row, and Kevin can do those."

As each bit of writing became clear, they would read the name aloud.

There were Woodruffs who must have been their great-grandparents, some who might have been Grandpa Woodruff's brothers, one Kevin decided after calculating dates had been a child of the great-grandparents.

"Makes you feel peculiar," Kevin said thoughtfully, looking for another stick because his original one had broken, "to know you're related to all these people, and you never met any of them."

Rosie nodded, glad she wasn't the only one who felt that way.

"If Grandmother Woodruff were here, though, you'd expect her to be buried beside her husband, wouldn't you? And she isn't."

Rosie considered the implications of this. "Maybe she's in a rest home, like Aunt Maude. I forget which of them is the oldest."

Kevin was frowning. "No, Aunt Maude isn't Grandmother's sister, she's her aunt. Aunt Maude's way older."

Rosie dredged through her memory. Mama had said so little about her family! "I'm sure Grandmother had a sister. Didn't Mama say she and Aunt Marge used to be dressed alike when they were little, that the dresses sometimes came from Grandmother's sister?"

Kevin wasn't interested in how a bunch of females had been dressed. "I don't remember anything about that. You on the last one, Nate? Whose grave is that one?"

Nathan knelt with his face close to the marble slab he'd just scraped free of the grime of decades. "Who's Ellen Waxwell?"

"Never heard of her," Kevin said, but Rosie's brain immediately went into high gear.

"That's her! Grandmother's sister! I'm sure her sister's name was Ellen. Aunt Maude and Mama talked about her once, when they didn't know I was around. The family disapproved of her because she was an actress—not in the movies, but on the stage—all except Grandmother. When the sister came home to visit, she bought presents for Mama and Aunt Marge."

"Oh." Kevin wasn't interested in Grandmother's sister,

either. "Well, I guess that's the last of them. If Grandmother died, she isn't buried here with the rest of the family."

Nathan stood up, brushing damp earth off the knees of his jeans. "Why don't we go explore the house?"

"Explore it?" Rosie felt a rush of horror, followed by uneasy excitement. "Would we dare?"

"Why not, if it's empty?" Kevin agreed. "It's not like it belongs to strangers. I mean, even if we didn't know them, they were relatives." He paused to relatch the rusty gate, his tone thoughtful. "I wonder who the place belongs to now? Even if Grandmother died without a will leaving it to Mama and Aunt Marge . . . or Aunt Maude . . . it would have to go to someone, wouldn't it?"

"Someone would have to keep paying taxes on it," Rosie said. Mrs. Kovacs had recently talked about taxes. "Or else the state would get it, I think."

They made their way back along the overgrown path toward the garden, speculating about ownership of the property. "Wouldn't it be neat if it was ours?" Kevin asked. "If—when Mama gets well, we could come here to live, maybe. We could raise our own food. I think that was the roof of a barn over beyond the garden. Maybe we could even raise chickens and cows."

Rosie was glad to emerge into the sunshine in the tangled garden, but from here she could see the faded bricks of the back of the house through the screening trees. "Are we really going to explore the house?"

"Let's see if it's locked," Kevin countered. "If we can get in without breaking in, why not?"

Halfway across the yard, Rosie thought something moved above her head. She stopped still, looking upward.

To Grandmother's House We Go

There was a window with a lacy curtain there, on the end of the wing, opposite where the fire had been; had it moved?

Prickles formed on the back of her neck as she stood there, watching. Maybe the window was broken; she couldn't really tell. Maybe a breeze had stirred the curtain.

Yet there seemed to be no breeze at ground level. Except for the drone of a bee somewhere close by, the silence was unbroken, the air completely still.

Something brushed against her ankle.

Rosie yipped in terror, then looked down and laughed at herself.

"What's wrong?" Kevin asked, turning as he started up the wooden steps to the covered veranda.

Rosie laughed shakily. "It's just a kitten. It rubbed against me and for a minute I thought—" She didn't finish, instead scooping up a half-grown gray and white cat to cuddle it against her chest. "Where did you come from?" she asked, looking into its soft furry face.

"Probably wandered over from the neighbors'," Kevin said, and went on up the steps. A moment later, with Nathan and Rosie a dozen yards behind him, he turned with a wide smile. "Hey! It's unlocked!"

At the same moment, Rosie glanced upward again.

This time there was no mistaking the movement.

A face stared down at her from that upstairs window, and Rosie felt as if her feet had grown roots there in the unmowed grass. Several seconds passed before the lace curtain dropped once more into place.

Rosie opened her mouth but her throat had closed and her tongue refused to work.

And Kevin was already disappearing into the house.

7

"COME ON, ROSIE!" NATHAN CALLED over his shoulder as he ran up the steps. "Let's see what's inside!"

Rosie stared up at the window for a moment, but the curtain hung limply. Her brothers had already vanished into the house, thinking it was deserted.

But it wasn't empty, she thought wildly. Someone—Grandmother?—still lived here. She had to stop the boys before the occupant caught them.

Her athletic shoes thumped across the wooden floor of the veranda, her heart thumping right along with her feet. Nathan had left the door open and she poked her head around the edge of it, calling out urgently.

"Kevin, wait! There's somebody here, upstairs! I saw her!"

Kevin was well along the corridor that ran from the back toward the front of the house. At the far end, like a light at the end of a tunnel, she could see a round window in the front door, through which dim light filtered.

"Kevin!" she hissed, and both boys stopped and turned around.

"What?"

Rosie took several steps toward them so she wouldn't have to shout.

"The house hasn't been abandoned! I saw someone at an upstairs window! We've got to get out of here, and knock!"

Kevin gave a startled glance upward, as if he could see through the ceiling, then trotted quickly back toward her, with Nathan moving ahead of him.

"You sure?"

"Of course I'm sure!" Without thinking, very tense, Rosie squeezed the kitten she still carried until it yowled and leaped free of her arms, streaking through one of the doors that opened to the side of the passageway.

Rosie let it go, spinning around to escape through the open doorway behind her, only to find her retreat cut off when a figure loomed before her.

For a moment she couldn't breathe.

"Who're you? What are you doing in my house?"

Was this Grandmother Woodruff?

Rosie skidded to a stop, feeling Nathan bump into her from behind.

The woman was taller than she'd expected. Much taller than Mama or Aunt Marge. And she didn't look anything like Mrs. Kovacs. Not smiling (nor looking as if she ever *did* smile) nor jolly nor plumply well-fed.

She was thin, with penetrating dark eyes that looked black in the dimly lit hallway and dark hair heavily streaked with gray. Her mouth was nicely shaped but at the moment compressed into a flat and unfriendly line.

Rosie tried to speak and couldn't. Her heart felt as if it would pound its way right through the wall of her chest.

Nathan was the one who found his tongue first. "Are you

our grandmother?'' he asked, sounding more like a frog than ever.

She seemed startled, both by the question and by his voice. "Your grandmother?" she echoed. Then she reached back and swung the door all the way open to let in more light and moved to one side so that the sun could reach in to touch their faces.

For a few moments it seemed to Rosie that a variety of conflicting emotions were mirrored in the woman's face, but perhaps that was only because the sun was behind her and her own face did not show up clearly. For when she spoke, her tone was harsh.

"Who are you? What do you want?"

Again Rosie tried to speak and failed. What was the matter with her? Why had she been stricken dumb?

"We . . . we're your grandchildren," Kevin said, sounding almost as peculiar as Nathan usually did. "If you're Mrs. Woodruff, I mean."

"My grandchildren!" Shock and disbelief were clear now; Rosie didn't imagine that. After a rather long silence, during which Rosie felt the kitten again winding around her ankles, the woman studied them. Rosie began to hope rather desperately that this was *not* their grandmother.

Almost immediately that bubble burst. "Lila's children?" Grandmother was incredulous, and if she felt any joy at seeing them for the first time, she concealed it very well.

"Kevin, and Rosie, and Nathan," Kevin explained uneasily.

The flat mouth went even flatter. "What are you doing here?"

Rosie finally found her own voice, though it squeaked. "We're sorry we came into the house. We . . . we thought nobody was living here anymore. It looked empty. . . ."

Her voice trailed off as she realized what a criticism that was of the appearance of the place.

Grandmother obviously took it that way.

"Nobody here well enough to cut grass and prune trees, or even keep the garden," she snapped.

It was only then that Rosie realized that her grandmother was using a walker, one of those metal frames like Great Aunt Maude used in the nursing home to hold onto when she walked so that she wouldn't fall.

"We . . . we're sorry for just walking in. Kevin thought everyone had moved away."

"I've lived here for forty years," Grandmother said. "Used to be able to work in the garden, drive the tractor, milk cows. I don't get outside the house anymore. Now I have heart trouble and arthritis, and since George broke his hip, he can't do it either."

"Who's George?" Nathan asked in the little puddle of silence that followed that statement.

"My brother-in-law. Your grandfather's brother, George Woodruff." She was staring at them in a way that reminded Rosie of the witch in Hansel and Gretel, as if she were evaluating them for their food value before she put them into the oven. Rosie swallowed hard.

"How did you get here? Where's Lila?" No friendliness, Rosie thought in despair. No welcome. Only hostility and suspicion.

"Mama's in the hospital," Kevin offered. "She had a stroke, and they said she'd be there a long time."

There was no change that Rosie could detect in the rigid face of the woman with the walker.

"They were going to put us in foster homes," Nathan said, "all different ones. We decided to run away, because we want to stay together."

"So you came here." There was astonishment in the words. "Well, I can't keep you. You'll have to go back."

Rosie's heart sank. Her voice wavered, but she managed to speak. "We can't. We don't have any money for bus fare." She was determined not to cry, and she bit down hard on her lower lip.

A gentle tapping sound made them all turn around to where an elderly man had just stepped through one of the doorways into the hall. The tapping sound came from a cane, one with three little legs coming out in different directions on the bottom of it.

"What's going on here?" the man asked.

"They're Lila's children," Grandmother said without taking her eyes off their faces. "She sent them here for me to take care of, can you imagine?"

"No!" Kevin and Rosie protested at the same time. "She doesn't know! She's too sick to know!"

"We came because we didn't want to be split up, and we couldn't think of anywhere else to go!"

This must be George. What would he be, their great-uncle? Rosie studied him, hoping against hope, because so far he seemed neutral, not hostile.

He was older than Grandmother, with white hair and bushy white eyebrows. His eyes, a faded blue in a tanned face, seemed even to twinkle a little.

"Lila's kids," he said. "Looks a little like Lila when she

was a little girl, don't she? The girl, I mean. What's your name, child?"

"Rosie. I mean Rosalie. They call me Rosie."

"Of course they do. And how about you fellers? What's your names?"

"Kevin."

"Nathan."

At the sound of Nathan's voice, Uncle George's eyebrows went up. "My, my. They musta dropped you in the bottom of a well, some time or other. Had a Jersey calf once, got separated from his mama right after he was born, stood all night in the creek under the bridge before I found him. Bawled and bawled for her, but the bank was too steep for him to get out. He sounded just about like you, so hoarse I could hardly hear him when I finally figured out where he was."

Uncle George sounded much more friendly than Grandmother did. Rosie decided to appeal to him.

"We can't go back to Summerville. We stowed away in a horse trailer to get here, and we haven't any money to go back. Besides, they'll separate us, put us in different foster homes."

She waited hopefully for Uncle George to evaluate this. He had sounded as if he remembered their mother with some affection.

Grandmother didn't give him time to think it over and perhaps suggest that they be allowed to stay. "We can't keep them. Is there enough money to buy bus tickets to get them back to Illinois?"

Uncle George scratched his head the way cartoon characters do when they're thinking. "Don't know what bus tickets cost these days, haven't been out of Nettleford on a bus in fifteen years, I guess. All the way to Summerville, though, and three of 'em . . . guess it wouldn't be cheap. I doubt we could do it today."

"We can't keep them," Grandmother repeated. "Not here."

Uncle George nodded his head a little, as if agreeing with her, though he had begun to smile. "After the first of the month, when our Social Security checks come, we could maybe afford bus tickets."

"That's four days!" Grandmother objected. She was looking at him in a most peculiar way, Rosie thought. What was the big deal about four days, when they had a house big enough to sleep a small army? Or was it that they didn't have any money to feed them? Guilt twisted at her, but she was still hoping they wouldn't be turned out immediately. The raspberries had helped some, but she knew Nathan would be starving before long. Nathan was always starving.

Uncle George spoke softly. "Four days. We can manage for that long, Dorothy. Between us."

Rosie hadn't known her grandmother's name was Dorothy. It didn't fit her; Dorothy was a little girl with a dog called Toto who went to Oz. Grandmother was more like the Wicked Witch of the West.

Something passed between Grandmother and Uncle George, something without words but so powerful that Rosie sensed the intensity of it. Did Grandmother hate her daughter so much that she could not even bear to see that daughter's children? Why? Rosie wondered. What could Mama possibly have done, as a child herself, to cause such animosity?

"Don't worry," Uncle George said, still gently. "I'll see to everything. Four days, is all. We can't turn them out on the road."

"Four days, then. In the meantime, we'd better call and tell someone where they are," Grandmother said. "Someone is worrying about them by this time."

"No," Rosie said, "we left a note, telling them we'd be all right! Don't call! You wouldn't be able to get Mama, anyway. She's in the hospital!"

If she called, would the social services people come after them?

Grandmother gave her a speaking look—she was good at speaking looks, it appeared—and, taking a good grip on the bars of her walker, clumped away. Presumably toward the telephone.

Rosie and Kevin exchanged a look that said a lot, too. So much for their hope of a refuge here.

Uncle George was smiling openly now. "Well, well," he said. "It's been a long time since we've had young ones in this house."

Nathan was less intimidated than Rosie and Kevin. "We're going to stay? At least until you get your checks? Can we have something to eat, then? We don't have much of anything left in our knapsacks."

Uncle George laughed. "That's what I remember best about youngsters. They're always hungry. Bottomless pits, my mother used to call us, Albert and me. Albert was your grandfather, you know. He was younger, like you," he tapped Nathan's shoulder with one veined old hand, "and he was always getting into trouble. I got the blame, because Ma used to say I was old enough to know better." He shook his head. "That was a very long time ago. Well, come along, let's see what we can find to eat."

He moved slowly, using the three-legged cane. "Fractured my hip early in the spring," he explained as they followed him into a big, old-fashioned kitchen. "Bones heal slow when you get to be my age. Got a steel pin right in here, you see." He patted his right thigh. "Still bothers me some. It's hard to bend my leg enough to get down and work in a garden the way I used to. Lucky we had stuff left from last year. Had to let the grass grow, too. Mower broke down, just like me." He chuckled as if this were amusing.

Rosie stared around the big room. The trees didn't press in closely at the back of the house, and the kitchen windows let in plenty of sunlight.

There was an old-fashioned wood range; she'd only seen them in pictures. There was an electric stove, too, but it looked almost as old as the wood range. The refrigerator was small and had rounded edges on the top. The table in the middle of the room was round and covered with a plastic tablecloth; a glass fruit jar held a spray of red bud. There were two coffee mugs and a few toast crumbs, as if someone had not yet cleaned up from breakfast.

"Let's see, here," Uncle George said, washing his hands at the longest sink Rosie had ever seen. The pipes made groaning sounds when he turned on the water. "What have we got to last three hungry kids until the soup's done for lunch?"

Rosie became aware then of the aroma from the steaming kettle on the electric stove. Her mouth watered. They were going to be fed and given a place to sleep for at least four nights and maybe—just maybe—they might be allowed to stay longer than that, when Grandmother fully understood the situation.

"Sit down, sit down," Uncle George said quite cheerfully. "How about bread and jelly? Blackberry jelly, this is." He brought a big jar to the table as they took seats. "How are you at slicing bread, young lady?" he asked Rosie, handing her a long knife and a plastic-wrapped loaf.

It was homemade bread, and she'd never cut any in her life, but Rosie gave it a try. Nobody said anything about it not being cut evenly. It was made with cracked-wheat flour, and the slices were thick and crusty.

Uncle George set out a plastic tub of margarine. "No real butter anymore," he apologized. "Old Sadie died last fall. I can't get down to milk a cow anyway, so maybe it was just as well, but I miss my real butter. Let's see. Milk? You all drink milk? It's two percent, not like what old Sadie gave."

The bread and jam were delicious. Rosie ate hungrily, beginning to feel better. Maybe something would work out yet so they wouldn't have to return to Summerville and go into foster homes.

Muffled thuds sounded in the hall just before Grandmother entered, the rubber-tipped legs on the walker announcing her progress. Rosie's stomach tightened again as Grandmother stood looking at them.

"I talked to your aunt Marge. She didn't even know you were missing. She said you've been staying with a Mrs. Kovacs."

Only Nathan kept on eating. Kevin and Rosie waited apprehensively.

"I told her I'd call her again when we put you on the bus," Grandmother said, "and she'll meet you."

The children said nothing. What was there to say?

"You're to do exactly what you're told while you're here," Grandmother said. "You can't go wandering around the house. We had a bad fire, years ago, and that wing's never been repaired. It's not safe, so we keep it locked up."

They stared at her.

"There are places where you could fall through the floors."

Still they said nothing. Nathan reached for another slice of bread.

"We're not used to children," Grandmother said, as if they hadn't noticed that by now. "Just two old people living in a falling-down house. We're not set up to have children." She turned to her brother-in-law. "George, you and I have to have a conference."

"Sure thing," Uncle George agreed. "Let's go sit in the parlor. These kitchen chairs are hard on old bones."

Rosie's heart began to pound again. She waited a moment after they'd left the room, then tiptoed to the door to peek into the corridor. The two were nowhere in sight.

"They're lying," she said quietly, staying in the doorway so that she would know if they came back unexpectedly. "They aren't alone in the house. I saw someone in the upstairs window."

Kevin licked jam off one thumb. "You saw Grandmother, or was it Uncle George?"

"Neither one of them. It was on the second floor, in the burned-out wing. A woman, I'm pretty sure it was a woman. Well, I *think* it was. I didn't really see the face very clearly. But I know there's someone else up there. And there wasn't time for anyone to come downstairs between when I saw the face and we met Grandmother and Uncle George down here. It has to be somebody different."

"Aw, Rosie, why would they lie? It's their house. They can have anybody in it they want to. It's none of our business. You must have seen the curtain blowing and imagined a face. There's nobody here but us and them."

"There is," Rosie said fiercely, and then stopped, listening.

Directly overhead, they heard the sound of footsteps and creaking boards.

8 THEY WAITED IN THE KITCHEN FOR Grandmother and Uncle George to return.

Nathan chewed methodically; Kevin had already eaten his fill. Rosie had simply lost her appetite after one sandwich.

There were no more sounds from overhead. After a while Kevin cleared his throat and spoke softly. "One of them must have gone upstairs. That's what we heard."

Rosie shook her head vigorously. "No. They were both in that room down the hall. Nobody went upstairs! There's someone else up there."

"There are three rocking chairs on the back porch," Nathan said thoughtfully, and paused to drain his milk glass. "Why would they have three chairs if only two people live here?"

"For when company comes," Kevin said, but Rosie looked around the room.

"Does this look like a place where they have company? We thought the house was abandoned, and it almost looks like it even inside. They don't do any entertaining, that's for sure. There's dust on everything, and nobody's washed the windows for ages." Mama was a stickler for clean windows, and when she was too busy to wash them herself, she asked Kevin and Rosie to do them.

"They can't," Kevin said at once. "Uncle George broke his hip, and Grandmother has something wrong with her so she has to use the walker. And it doesn't sound as if they have much money. I doubt if they could hire anyone to help."

Rosie spoke with quiet conviction. "There's someone else living here. Upstairs. We heard someone walking around."

Nathan had finished eating and he wiped his mouth with a paper napkin, leaving purplish stains of blackberry jam. "Remember, I said the house looked haunted? Maybe it's a ghost."

Rosie was scornful. "A ghost wouldn't make noises when it walked. And it was a real face I saw in the window."

"What did it look like?" Kevin asked. "Old or young? A man's face, or a woman's?"

Rosie *knew* she'd seen a face. The trouble was, it had been only for a matter of seconds, and it was high overhead, partially obscured by a lace curtain. "I don't know for sure. Old, I think. A woman."

They were still thinking about it when Grandmother and Uncle George came back. Uncle George was smiling, as if he were enjoying this unexpected company. Grandmother looked as if she'd just swallowed one of those bitter-tasting bugs out of the garden.

"I think I'll have another cup of coffee first," Uncle

George said, lifting the pot off the stove, "and then I'll get about my chores."

"We'll help," Kevin offered.

"No, no, nothing for young ones to do," Uncle George said. "Not right now, anyway."

"You might as well make yourselves useful, though," Grandmother said. "The raspberries are ripe enough to pick. There are buckets in the pantry." She gave Uncle George a look that said something important, although Rosie couldn't tell what it was. She thought Uncle George knew, though; he nodded ever so slightly.

Mama and Daddy used to "talk" that way, Rosie thought. Without words, simply looking at each other; often their eyes had sparkled with hidden mischief, and she had envied their closeness as well as been glad it was there, because it made her feel warm and secure and happy.

It seemed a long time since she'd felt secure and happy.

Grandmother's walker made subdued thumps as she crossed to a door and opened it, emerging with small plastic pails that had once held peanut butter. It was awkward for her, carrying them by the handles as she gripped the bars of the walker.

"Here," she said. "There's time to fill all of these before lunch. Two for each of you."

Uncle George chuckled. "Better put some more water in the soup, so we'll have enough to go around."

Grandmother, Rosie decided uncomfortably, appeared not to have much of a sense of humor. "A few more potatoes and carrots would be more to the point. You," Grandmother said, looking at Kevin, "can pull some carrots. There are a few coming up in the far corner; the carrots went to seed last year and started over by themselves, or we wouldn't have any."

"Okay," Kevin agreed, accepting one of the yellow plastic buckets.

"Bring them right back; they take a while to cook."

"Yes, ma'am," Kevin said.

When they'd let themselves out onto that back veranda, Uncle George closed the door firmly behind them.

The boys went down the steps, heading for the overgrown garden, but Rosie hesitated, looking around. She felt strange, and she wasn't sure why. It was more than being in an unfamiliar house, among people who didn't welcome them. People who lied to them.

Surely she hadn't imagined seeing a face in that upstairs window. And all three of them had heard the sounds over the kitchen, which was directly under the area where a person might be who'd looked down on them a few minutes earlier.

There *were* three rocking chairs. *Not an extra one for a visitor,* Rosie insisted silently; they didn't have that many visitors, if they had any at all. The rockers were wooden, and each had a faded cushion on the seat. As if the inhabitants of the house, three of them, sat out here in the cool of the evening, rocking together.

Rosie inhaled deeply and went on down the steps after her brothers. The back of her neck prickled, but she resisted looking back to see if anyone watched from that upstairs window.

Later, though, after Kevin had taken a bunch of fat orange carrots to the house and returned to join the others in picking berries, Rosie couldn't help sneaking glances toward that window. There was nothing there, only the limp lace curtain.

There were lots of raspberries. The three filled their buckets fairly quickly, not talking much.

Once Nathan said, "This wouldn't be a bad place to live. It's nice here in the country."

"They don't want us," Rosie reminded him softly.

Nathan's sigh was deep. "I miss Mama," he said after a moment of silence.

"We all do," Kevin assured him, and Rosie's eyes stung with the tears that seemed to be so close to the surface these days. "But we're together; we have each other. And maybe by the time school starts, Mama will be home again."

They didn't actually have a home anymore, Rosie thought. Not a *place.* But if Mama got well—*when* she got well—they would all be together again, somewhere. Maybe Mrs. Kovacs would still have an apartment she could rent to them. Then they'd be a family again.

Rosie wished, quite desperately, that it would happen soon.

She had filled her second bucket, so she set it aside and helped Nathan finish filling his. When she retrieved her own pails, she saw that Kevin was staring through the trees toward what was visible of a roof off beyond a row of untrimmed shrubs.

"I wonder if they'd care if we explored the barn," he said. "It looks interesting. It's too bad they don't still have a cow, and horses, and chickens."

Nathan looked around thoughtfully at the garden, untended except for one small patch of flowers that was relatively free of weeds. "I wonder what Uncle George's chores are. He didn't even come outside."

72

"He probably helps keep house, since Grandmother doesn't get around very well," Kevin said. "Come on, let's take these inside. Maybe lunch is ready."

Rosie liked it better out in the sunshine than in the shadowy house, but she, too, was getting hungry again.

She stepped closer to the flower bed—a colorful display of blooms she didn't recognize, except for some lilies of the valley that were almost hidden under the edge of a bush bearing pink roses. Someone had cared enough about beauty to care for these, even if they hadn't planted or weeded the vegetables this year. Grandmother, or Uncle George? Or, the thought came without warning, after she'd almost forgotten about it, had it been the *other* person in the house?

Instinctively, her gaze swung upward to that window in the partially burned wing of the house, and there it was again.

The face. Too far away to see clearly, but unmistakably a face.

The person stared for long moments while Rosie's mouth went dry; she couldn't even call out to her brothers, who had already started for the house, so that they would see it, too.

And then, quite deliberately, the lace curtain was dropped back into place, and the face was hidden.

It wasn't gone, though, Rosie thought, her heart thudding audibly in her chest. Behind the curtain, the mysterious inhabitant still stood, watching her.

Rosie suddenly broke free of the spell that had held her, running so that a few of the raspberries spilled out of her buckets to catch the boys at the bottom of the steps.

"I saw it again, the face," Rosie gasped, as Kevin turned

toward her. "There is someone else here, there is!"

Kevin's eyes rolled upward, as if he could see through the roof of the veranda and around the corner to the window. "It was probably one of them—Grandmother or Uncle George—checking to see if we were finished yet," he said uncertainly.

But when they entered the kitchen a moment later, Grandmother and Uncle George were both there.

"See?" Rosie mouthed at her brother when Grandmother had taken the berries to put on the edge of the sink, and Uncle George had turned his back to stir the soup. "There's someone else!"

Kevin licked his lips, and for a moment *they* were doing it, speaking without words. What was going on? Why would Grandmother and Uncle George act as if the two of them lived here alone if they didn't?

And then Uncle George was directing them to take seats at the table while he ladled out the soup, and Grandmother was slicing more of the chewy homemade bread, and they were ready to eat.

Rosie was hungry, and the bread and soup were delicious. She ate in silence, scarcely hearing Nathan as he asked questions about the animals they had had in the old days, and her mind grappled with the mystery.

Who lived upstairs, and why was it a secret?

9 AT THE END OF THE MEAL, UNCLE George brought out a big pan with a flat cake in it, with one piece missing. "Young ones always like cake, don't they?" he asked, smiling.

"We do," Nathan assured him, assessing the size of the empty space where the first piece had been removed. Rosie knew he was thinking that it had been a very *small* piece. Nathan liked to be allowed to cut his own size piece, which was never small at all.

Uncle George was cutting it, though. And to Nathan's relief, written clearly on his owl-like face, the chunks were generous.

"Carrot cake," Uncle George said as he served them. "With cream cheese frosting."

Nathan quickly took a bite, then hesitated when Uncle George put plastic wrap back over the cake. "Aren't you going to have some?"

"No, I don't have much of a sweet tooth anymore," Uncle George said. "Fruit now, I like fruit. And jam. Dorothy makes wonderful jam."

Rosie slid a glance at Grandmother. Uncle George hadn't offered her any cake, either. It made Rosie feel peculiar to hear Grandmother called Dorothy. As if she were young, Rosie thought, and a regular person instead of . . .

Instead of what? She concentrated, outwardly, on the thick, moist cake, enjoying the spicy flavor and the chewy raisins. Inwardly, though, she couldn't help thinking about Grandmother.

Why had she given away her children to her aunt when the girls were no older than Rosie and Nathan were now? How could a mother do that? She hadn't even gone to visit them for years or written to them or sent presents, Rosie knew, because she'd heard her mother and Aunt Marge talking about it one day when they didn't know she was listening. It had hurt them very much, and even after they were grown they didn't understand.

The thought came so swiftly that Rosie almost lost her appetite: *Mama had signed papers that would allow the social services people to put them into foster homes.*

But Mama loved them, Rosie thought, fighting back sudden tears. She *did!* She'd proved it over and over again, struggling to keep the family together after Daddy died. And she always did the best she could to make birthdays and Christmas wonderful days, even if they didn't have much money. There was always a decorated cake—Mama was very clever about making trains or racing cars out of cakes, and once one with a ballerina on it for Rosie—and songs and laughter.

The tears threatened to overflow as Rosie remembered. Mama was sick, terribly sick, and maybe she thought she was going to die. Only something that serious could make her sign papers saying someone else could take her children.

She couldn't bear to think about Mama any more right now, or about being separated from her brothers. Rosie swallowed hard. It would be easier to think about Grandmother, who had risen from the table and was running water in the sink to wash the dishes.

Grandmother's back was stiff and straight when she wasn't leaning on her walker. Rosie blinked away the moisture from her eyes and forced herself to take another bite of cake just as Nathan asked, "Aren't you going to have any cake, Grandmother?"

"Not now," Grandmother said shortly, as if it were a frivolous question.

Uncle George was putting the cake back in the pantry, and neither he nor Grandmother faced the children. Kevin looked startled, then leaned closer to Rosie to whisper.

"If neither of them has a sweet tooth, why did they bake that big cake, and who ate the missing piece?"

"Maybe Grandmother just doesn't feel like cake right now," Rosie suggested uncertainly.

As if on cue, in response to his curiosity, there was a scraping sound overhead, as if someone had shoved a chair back from a table, perhaps. Grandmother, rinsing dishes at the sink, didn't appear to hear it.

Rosie put down her fork. *Someone* in this house liked sweets, and it wasn't either of the two adults here in the kitchen.

And then she noticed another peculiar thing. When Uncle George came out of the pantry, he locked the door with an old-fashioned key and dropped it into his pocket.

Kevin had noticed, too, and the look he and Rosie exchanged was heavy with meaning even though there were no words. What was going on?

It wasn't until the meal was finished and they'd been shooed outside and told to play in the sun for an hour or two while Grandmother rested that they realized Nathan, too, had been aware of the strangeness in the big, old house.

"Why do they lock up the food?" Nathan wanted to know. "I mean, they asked if we wanted more to eat, so they don't intend to starve us. Why do they lock it all in that funny little room?"

"The funny little room is a pantry," Rosie said. "It's a place to keep food when you don't have lots of cupboard space in the kitchen."

"I don't think they're locking it up to keep it away from *us*," Kevin said, and Rosie knew she hadn't been the only one speculating about this household. "I think it's because of . . . whoever it is who lives upstairs."

"Who is it?" Nathan wondered aloud.

Kevin shrugged, leading the way along a path that led toward the barn. "Who knows? If they're not going to let us stay here, I guess it's none of our business, anyway. Let's go explore the barn."

"But don't you wonder?" Rosie demanded. "Who is it? Why can't we meet them? Why do Grandmother and Uncle George lie about whoever it is?"

Kevin didn't answer, and the other two trotted along after him.

The barn was big and old and had a little moldy hay left

in it, and scurrying mice. There were stalls where horses had been kept once, long ago, and a manger where cows had been fed. The boys seemed to enjoy prowling around in it, but Rosie went back outside, where she couldn't stop thinking about how odd everything was about this place.

She also couldn't stop wondering what would happen when they were put on the bus and sent home to Summerville, which was no longer home at all.

It wasn't fun being a kid anymore, Rosie decided. It was awful to have grown people who didn't care anything about you making the decisions about your life. Even the ones who *did* care, like Mrs. Kovacs and Aunt Marge, didn't seem to have any power. It wasn't fair.

She was glad when the boys had seen enough of the barn and came back out into the sunshine.

They headed back to the house. "I saw a box of Chinese checkers on the porch that we can play, I guess," Kevin said, giving up on further exploration. They cut across what would have been a proper garden if anyone had replanted and tended it. Rosie paused at the flower bed, wondering again who had felt the flowers were important enough to weed when no one had bothered to plant any vegetables.

You'd think that people who didn't have much money, and had all this land, would produce something to eat rather than raise flowers to look at, she thought.

The lilies of the valley were in the shadiest spot, with tiny creamy-white bell-like blossoms. Rosie studied the other flowers, recognizing only the purple ones that looked as if they had little faces. Mama had once brought some home in a basket from the supermarket to set in a window box.

"If we ever have a house again," Mama had said early this

past spring, before she got sick, "I'm going to plant lots of pansies. They look like such cute, friendly little creatures."

They did look that way. But pansies didn't come up year after year, the way lily of the valley did; you had to plant them every year.

So who had planted these?

Someone who enjoyed their beauty, Rosie thought, but Grandmother's house didn't look as if anyone there cared about beauty. Rosie had glimpsed pictures on the walls, but they were old and faded and undusted.

An indentation in the damp earth near the lilies made her bend over to inspect it more closely. Someone had walked here recently, certainly since there had last been rain; there was a heel mark clearly imprinted between two plants.

A high heel, from a shoe like the ones Mama wore when she dressed up to go out. Only she hadn't done that very often since Daddy had died. Rosie sighed and straightened. She didn't care much about playing Chinese checkers, but there seemed little else to do. She followed her brothers toward the porch.

It wasn't until much later that afternoon, when Grandmother came clumping out with her walker to check on them as Uncle George served lemonade with tinkling ice in the glasses, that Rosie noticed Grandmother's shoes.

They were sturdy and black, with flat heels.

Most assuredly they had not made the heel print in the flower bed, Rosie thought.

So, she mused, unaware as Nathan jumped three of her marbles, she was right about the person upstairs being a woman. A woman who wore high heels even when she went into the garden. A woman who did not use a walker, for that, too, would have left prints in soft dirt.

"Thought you might be getting thirsty," Uncle George said, cheerful as always. He lingered after Grandmother had reentered the house, and Nathan asked a question that had been nagging at Rosie.

"Did you know my mother?"

"Your mother? Little Lila. Yes, I remember her. Not that I was around much when she was a little girl; I was away at sea most of the time. I was a sailor, you know. Traveled all around the world, I did, when I was young."

Uncle George eased a haunch onto the porch railing and half sat, half stood, facing them. He seemed good-natured, relaxed. Friendly.

Not like Grandmother, Rosie reflected. It was a pity it wasn't Uncle George's house instead of Grandmother's.

"Mama never mentioned you." Nathan had forgotten about playing Chinese checkers, and Kevin didn't prompt him. He, too, was curious about what had happened here all those years ago.

"I don't suppose she'd even remember me, really," Uncle George said. "She wasn't but four or five, I reckon, the last time I saw her."

"Why did Grandmother send her away?"

Rosie caught her breath. It ought to have occurred to her to warn Nathan about asking personal questions, because he often did it. Yet she wanted to know the answers, too.

For a moment she thought Uncle George wouldn't reply. He had a rather sad expression as he sighed and searched for words. "Some things are kind of hard to explain," he said at last. "But people have reasons for what they do. Even if they can't always tell you what they are."

Nathan's eyes were magnified through the thick glasses so they seemed enormous. "Did Mama do something really bad that made Grandmother not want her?"

Listening, Rosie felt her throat close. If he would only tell the truth, if the mystery could be explained so they would understand it . . .

But Uncle George only sighed again and slid onto both feet, reaching for his cane. "No, sonny, your ma never did anything bad. Nor her sister Marge, either. My goodness, it's getting late. It's time I put the roast on for supper or it won't be cooked on time."

"But then why—" Nathan began, only to stop when Uncle George shook his head.

"Some things are not my secrets to tell, boy. Some can't be explained at all. Tell you what, I think there might be some onions coming up from last year's seed, way back there in the corner nearest the barn. Why don't you see, and fetch me a few? We could have a salad with our roast and potatoes."

Miraculously, Nathan didn't tell him that he didn't like onions in his salad. He returned his attention to the game board and jumped another of Rosie's marbles.

Rosie was pretty sure she and Kevin hadn't even had their turns yet, but she said nothing. She didn't care about checkers.

Kevin stared after Uncle George's retreating figure. He'd forgotten the game, too. "Boy, talk about a weird place. I guess maybe I'll be glad to go back to Summerville, even if I don't know what's going to happen next."

He pushed back his chair. "I'll go look for the onions," he said, and went down the steps.

Rosie sat still, thinking furiously.

They might have to go back to Summerville, but before they did, she thought with determination, she was going to learn something.

She was going to find out who the mysterious person in the fire-damaged wing was, and maybe the explanations for some of the other peculiar things they'd noticed.

When she said as much to Nathan, her little brother shoved his glasses into place and dumped the marbles off the board.

"How do we start?" he asked.

10

THERE WAS NO ONE IN THE KITCHEN
when the trio reentered the house. They
moved quietly along the hallway toward that
dim window at the front of the house, for the
voices led them to where Grandmother and
Uncle George were.

The passageway was gloomy. The thickly clustered trees
that pressed in on all sides except directly behind them kept
out the sun. There was a stairway that rose to Rosie's left
as she walked; she glanced upward into an even deeper
gloom at the top of the steps, then stopped so suddenly that
Nathan stepped on her heels.

Rosie scarcely noticed because she was so intent on hearing what Grandmother was saying.

"Why did they have to come *now?* What are we going to
do?" They were in a parlor opposite the stairway. The door
was open, and she could see into the room, though Grandmother and Uncle George were out of sight.

The wallpaper was faded to a pale red background with
some sort of flowered pattern on it. There were old-

fashioned pictures on the bit of wall she could see, brownish photographs in heavy gold frames. One was of a stern-looking man with a brushy mustache and another was of an equally unsmiling woman with her hair drawn back into a bun; the woman had a high, stiff-looking collar held together with an elaborate jeweled pin.

Ancestors, no doubt. Rosie wondered if they had always been so sober, or only looked that way because the pictures had been taken so long ago, when it was necessary to sit very still for minutes at a time in order to have a photograph made.

It wasn't the pictures or the furnishings of the parlor that held Rosie's attention, however. It was the words that she heard.

"We're going to put them up for a few days, and then as soon as the checks come and I can get to the bank and cash them," Uncle George was saying, "I'll buy bus tickets and send them back where they came from."

"A few days," Grandmother repeated, sounding cross. "I suppose we'll have to put them in my bedroom to sleep. It's the only one on the ground floor that's habitable."

"And then where would you sleep?" Uncle George asked gently. "No, no, Dorothy. That doesn't make any sense. All your things are in your room, and we've neither of us enough energy to move them upstairs. Besides, you'd never get up and down with that walker without breaking your neck; you'd be too likely to fall."

"Well," Grandmother said, even more cross now, so that her displeasure registered clearly with the silent trio listening outside the parlor door, "we can't put them in *your* little cubbyhole. There's not room for three."

"There's not room for three in your room, either."
Uncle George spoke soothingly. "We can't put two boys
and that little girl all into your one bed."

"So what are we going to do? We can't put *them* upstairs!"

"Of course we can. That's just what we'll do. The rooms
are a little dusty, but children aren't likely to notice that. I'll
take up fresh sheets, and they can help me make up the
beds. They'll be as far from the east wing as we can get
them, and it will work out fine. Don't worry about it, Dorothy. I'll look after things, I promise you."

Rosie turned her head to look into Kevin's face, only a
couple of feet from her own. He, too, had a strained look.
It was painfully clear that Grandmother did not want
them here.

Nobody wanted them, Rosie thought sadly. Well, maybe
Mrs. Kovacs did, a little, but she couldn't keep them. Even
if the social services people would agree to it, Mrs. Kovacs
had to go to her sister's in Florida because the sister was
having an operation and would need someone to care for
her. And while Aunt Marge said she couldn't take three
kids because she had such a tiny apartment—which was
true—Rosie didn't think she really wanted them, either.
She'd even heard Aunt Marge say, once, to Mama, "I'm
glad it's you raising kids, not me. How do you stand the
noise they make?"

Mama had laughed, and it hadn't bothered Rosie at the
time because she had thought they would always be safe
with Mama. But she remembered it now.

Suddenly Rosie didn't want to hear anymore. She had
decided to play detective, which she supposed included

listening in on revealing conversations, but for the moment she couldn't bear to hear any more about how unwelcome they were.

She turned away, intending to retrace her steps to the covered veranda and wait there until Uncle George summoned them.

Kevin and Nathan silently followed her lead. But they had lingered long enough to hear Grandmother say, "You'd better check on them. Make sure they aren't poking around where they don't belong."

"They're playing checkers on the porch, having a good time. They're nice children, Dorothy, they really are."

"It doesn't matter how nice they are, does it?" Grandmother demanded, sounding so waspish that Rosie and Kevin again exchanged glances. "My own children were nice enough, but if I couldn't have them here, how can we have these three?"

Rosie fled, almost forgetting to be quiet. She felt like crying. In fact, she found when she emerged onto the veranda that she *was* crying; she scrubbed at her wet cheeks with her hands and wiped them on her jeans.

"If she thought Mama and Aunt Marge were nice," she said, choking, "why did she give them away?"

Nathan was unblinking. "I saw another flashlight in a drawer in the kitchen," he said. "We can use it tonight to investigate, too."

Rosie was overcome with a surge of emotion. She hugged him and made herself smile.

"The three detectives," she said. "Just like in the books."

Kevin, who was an avid reader of mysteries, nodded. "Whatever's going on, we'll find out," he said.

When Uncle George came out a few minutes later, they were once more playing Chinese checkers.

It was a good thing he couldn't hear her heart pounding, Rosie thought, not looking at him for fear her face would give her away. It had just occurred to her that if they went looking for the mysterious occupant of the east wing, the one that had been partially burned a long time ago, they might well come face to face with someone who didn't want to see them any more than Grandmother did.

Rosie didn't have a chance to talk to her brothers about plans for that night, and so she simply had to bottle up the apprehension that had begun to build inside her.

"Why don't we all go sit in the parlor?" Uncle George said, after they'd eaten a very good supper and the children had done the dishes. "Listen to some music on the radio."

Radio? Rosie thought. *Not TV?*

When they were ushered into the parlor where Grandmother had a rocking chair and Uncle George settled into a recliner, there was certainly no television. Yet Rosie distinctly recalled a drunken-looking antenna on the roof.

There was music on the radio—actually a surprising feature of the room, which otherwise looked as if it hadn't been changed in fifty years. It was a boom box very much like the one Kevin had been forced to leave behind at Mrs. Kovacs' house, the one that had belonged to Daddy before he died. It had been his present from Mama that last Christmas, and he'd said Kevin was to have it.

Grandmother had the radio tuned to a station that played classical music, which was all right. Mama liked that, too. Grandmother was knitting a slipper, pale pink with white angora trim.

Rosie settled onto the sofa, staring at the slipper. Who was it for? It was hard to imagine Grandmother wearing anything so delicate and pretty. Her gaze drifted down to Grandmother's feet in their sturdy dark shoes, in motion as she kept the chair rocking rhythmically.

No, Rosie decided. It wasn't for Grandmother. For one thing, the slipper looked too small, as well as delicate. For whom, then?

Kevin sat on one side of her, Nathan on the other side, and Rosie knew they were as uncomfortable as she was.

Nathan suddenly cleared his throat, and Rosie followed his gaze to a clutter of small pictures on the table beside Grandmother. The table also held a lamp and a Bible that looked well worn.

Did people who gave their children away, and didn't want to know their grandchildren, read the Bible?

And then Rosie saw the picture that had caught Nathan's attention, just as he asked, "Is that a picture of my mother?"

The creaking rocker stopped. Grandmother turned her head slowly, as if her neck were stiff. Rosie thought she must have forgotten that the photographs were there on the small table. Grandmother, too, cleared her throat.

"Oh, that one. Yes. That's Lila when she was"—for a moment her voice sounded as froggy as Nathan's— "three," she finished.

"How old was she when you sent her away?" Nathan asked.

On the radio an announcer broke in with a news brief. In the corner of the room a clock ticked loudly. Rosie thought Grandmother wasn't going to answer.

When she did, her voice was very low. "She was five, and Marjorie was nine, when they went to live with Aunt

Maude. They were better off there in Illinois, with Maude."

Rosie wanted to scream at her. *But they weren't! They were lonely and frightened and confused, and they never got over it! It still hurts them both, because they don't understand why you didn't want them!*

But of course Rosie couldn't say a thing.

Nathan, however, was not intimidated by this oppressive room, by the old woman who had begun to rock and knit again.

"Why?" he asked. "Why didn't you want them? Your own kids?"

When she turned her head to face them, the light reflected off her glasses so they couldn't see her eyes. Somehow that was disturbing to Rosie, as if Grandmother could see them, but they could not really see her.

"It wasn't that I didn't want them," Grandmother said heavily, and to Rosie's imagination it seemed that she got older before their eyes. "It was only that there was so much trouble here, and I knew they'd be better off with Aunt Maude. I couldn't . . . keep children in this house any longer."

"Is that when you got hurt, so you had to use the walker?" Nathan persisted.

Ordinarily, knowing he was being too nosy, Rosie would have pinched him to make him shut up, but she wanted to know the answer, too.

Grandmother's throat worked soundlessly, as if she intended to reply but couldn't.

It was Uncle George who spoke. "No, your grandmother had a fall, years after that time, and now arthritis in the places where the bones were broken makes her stiff.

That happens to a lot of us when we get older. It was a bad time, when Albert was killed. Did you know about that? It was a tractor accident. Rolled on him and crushed him. It was very hard for your grandmother."

"It was hard for Mama, too," Nathan countered, "when *our* daddy died. But she didn't give us away."

"Albert's accident wasn't the only thing that went wrong," Uncle George said, after a moment had passed and it was clear that Grandmother wasn't going to respond. She was no longer rocking, and the knitting lay motionless in her lap as she stared across the room at nothing.

Uncle George hesitated, looking at her, then continued. "We had a real bad fire, you know. Maybe you noticed the smoke damage, there in the east wing. It didn't burn down the whole wing—or the whole house—because it was brick, but a lot of the inside burned. Your great-aunt Ellen died in the fire. I don't suppose you know anything about her."

Kevin found his voice. "We saw her tombstone in the little cemetery."

"That's right. She and your grandmother were sisters, same as Lila and Marjorie were. Well, she was burned to death. It was a terrible time. And with Albert gone, there was nobody to work the farm. I came home on leave, but I had to go back to sea, and I wasn't much of a farmer, anyway. There wasn't a lot of money for a while. Not enough to take care of a family. Your grandmother just couldn't handle things here, with children and all, so she let Maude take them. It was better that way."

Words flooded Rosie's mind, although she was unable to speak them. Maybe Grandmother had needed to send Mama and Aunt Marge to Aunt Maude for a little while, but why had she never taken them back? Why hadn't she even written to them, or gone to visit them?

Rosie knew by looking at Kevin's face that he was thinking the same things.

Nathan would probably have asked more questions, but Grandmother suddenly put aside the pink slipper, and by lifting herself on the arms of the rocker she stood up. "I'm going to get out sheets and blankets. I don't think any were left upstairs," she said, and grasping the bars on her walker she left the room.

It was far too early, Rosie thought, to be making up beds. Grandmother just didn't want to talk about any of these things anymore.

Nathan turned to Uncle George, no doubt to continue trying to pry information out of him, but Uncle George immediately diverted his attention.

"If I'm not mistaken," he said, "there are some old pictures of your mother when she was a little girl, in that album there on the bottom shelf of the table. Why don't you have a look at them, eh?"

He got up and put the dusty black album on Nathan's knees. "I'll just go along and talk to your grandmother. It upsets her to talk about the bad things that happened, all those years ago. She and her sister Ellen, who died in the fire, were very close. It might be better if you didn't mention any of this again, all right?"

None of the trio on the couch replied to this, but he seemed to take it for granted that they would do as he asked and stop poking into Grandmother's past.

Uncle George's cane made little tapping sounds as he moved away from them along the uncarpeted hallway.

From the radio the announcer said, "Tomorrow's forecast calls for rain, perhaps heavy by tomorrow night, clearing by Saturday. And now we return to our evening concert with a recording of Hungarian Rhapsodies by Franz Liszt."

The clock ticked loudly in its corner.

Nathan opened the big photograph album on his lap and began to turn the pages, stopping when he came to a snapshot of someone he recognized.

"That's Mama. And that's Aunt Marge. Aunt Maude had the same pictures in her album."

There were others, most of them marked with names and dates. "Mama looks a lot like you, Rosie," Nathan said thoughtfully, touching the snapshot with his fingers. When Rosie glanced up at his face, she saw tears behind his glasses.

"I guess it's me who looks like her," she managed, and hugged him against her.

They worked their way through all the faded old pictures, in black and white or the brown called sepia, and saw what Grandmother had looked like as a young woman, in a housedress and an apron and also dressed up to go to church, maybe. Even in those days, Rosie noted, she had worn sensible clothes, sensible shoes.

And there were pictures of Aunt Maude as a young woman, and of their grandfather, Albert, and many people they didn't know. And then, taking up an entire page, a professional photograph, not a snapshot, of a strikingly pretty young woman in a fancy dress with fluffy blond hair and a fur piece around her neck.

"Is it Grandmother?" Nathan asked, puzzled, referring back to the previous page for comparison, for there was no

name written below this picture. "It's like her, but not
. . . quite."

Kevin reached over to slip the photograph out of the
little corner pieces that held it and read what was written
on the back. "No, it says Ellen Waxwell. Grandmother's
sister."

Rosie heard her own voice, hollow, echoing. "The one
who was killed in the fire in the east wing."

They studied the lovely, merry face. Aunt Ellen looked
so happy. Had Grandmother ever looked that happy,
before Grandfather and her sister died?

But Rosie didn't have time to dwell on it, because Nathan turned the page, and they all caught their breaths.

Because here, on the last few pages of the album, were
the pictures they would never have expected to see. Not in
this house, in Grandmother's album.

Beside her, Kevin swallowed audibly, and Rosie sat as if
turned to a statue.

Nathan's mouth sagged open. For long moments they sat
there, looking in disbelief at pictures they had never before
seen, of their mother and Aunt Marge when they were little
girls in school, and then teenagers, long after they had gone
to live with Aunt Maude. But more astonishing were other
pictures that followed, pictures they *did* recognize.

Rosie jumped when they heard the tap of Uncle George's
cane, the *thump, thump* of Grandmother's walker.

Quickly, knowing it would not do to be caught looking
at *these* pictures, Rosie closed the book and shoved the
album back onto the shelf.

How had pictures of herself and Kevin and Nathan come
to be here among the mementos of a grandmother who had

never met them or shown the slightest interest in them?

It was all very strange, and it had a powerful effect on Rosie. Her resolution about investigating, which had been wavering, was back, stronger than ever.

Whatever the mystery was, she thought, they were going to solve it. Whether Grandmother let them stay or not, before they went back to Summerville they were going to have some answers.

Uncle George's arms were heaped with blankets and sheets.

"Come along," he said, "and before it gets any later—your grandmother and I go to bed rather early, I'm afraid—we'll get you settled in your rooms. Then we'll have some cocoa with marshmallows, how about that?"

Bemused, hardly thinking about what he said, Rosie followed the others out of the parlor and up the stairs that rose into near darkness above them, leaving Grandmother behind.

11

THERE WAS STILL PLENTY OF DAYLIGHT outside. Rosie glimpsed it through various windows that obviously had not been washed in years. But here inside the house it was so dark that she could barely see her surroundings when she reached the top of the stairs.

They followed Uncle George with his armload of bedding to the right, toward the west wing. Behind them, the corridor vanished in gloom. Ahead, between rows of closed doors, they could make out their way after Uncle George had turned on the dim overhead light.

Nathan reached for Rosie's hand, and she squeezed his reassuringly, though it looked pretty spooky to her, too.

Uncle George, however, talked on cheerfully as they went. "Big old place, isn't it? It was full when I was a boy. Did you know I was born here, and so was your grandfather, Albert? Right in this house! People didn't have their babies in hospitals in those days; they got born at home. We had aunts and cousins—and grandparents—all living with us. Always somebody to play with, if there was any time to play. This was a working farm then, and there were so many chores to do, even when we were Nathan's age, that play time was a special treat."

Nathan was wide-eyed. "You mean you had to work all the time?"

"Well, near enough. We always wished we lived nearer the Mississippi, so we could have a more authentic background to play Tom Sawyer and Huckleberry Finn. They still read Mark Twain in school, do they?"

Kevin was the one who replied. "Not in school, but Mama read us those books at home."

Uncle George nodded. "Good stuff! We didn't have the big river, so we had to make do with that little old creek on the back of the place. I remember going out there with Ma in the spring when the violets were blooming along the banks, when I wasn't but about three or four years old. We were forbidden to go there alone then. I guess I was about nine or ten when we discovered a big cave there. It was every bit as good as the one Mark Twain wrote about. We always wanted to spend the night in it—or we thought we did, though I wouldn't be surprised if we'd have come high-tailing it home when it got full dark—but Ma wouldn't let us sleep outside at night. And we had to get up early and bring in the cows and feed stock before breakfast."

One of the blankets he carried was trailing, and he paused to rearrange it. "Hope I didn't get it too dirty. Floor hasn't been vacuumed in a while. Dorothy used to keep it cleaned even if there wasn't anybody sleeping up here, before she got so she had to use the walker. Then she hired somebody to come in a couple times a year so the dust didn't get too thick. But there hasn't been anybody in to do it since last fall, if I remember right. Costs a bunch to get the whole house cleaned, and there didn't seem to be any particular reason to do it."

They came to the end of the straight part of the hall and turned to the left, into the west wing.

"The rooms back here are in the best shape," Uncle George told them, flipping another switch to turn on another of the dim bulbs. "We didn't have electric lights up here when I was your age. That's what those little tables were for, the kerosene lamps we carried up. Then we got those pump-up gas lanterns, and they seemed wonderful, the amount of light they gave. I remember when my ma— that'd be your great-grandma—finally talked Grandpa into putting in electricity. My, didn't we think we were fancy when we first got those lights! They seemed brighter in those days than they do now." He paused and threw open a door on the right. "Feel around there for the switch, will you, Kevin? There was a time when I thought we'd ought to put some bigger bulbs up here, but with nobody much left living here, it didn't seem worth the effort. There we go."

The overhead light came on, illuminating an old-fashioned room with a high bed (with four posters, yet, Rosie noted) and windows high enough to be above the trees.

"I thought we'd put Rosie in here, and you boys right next door," Uncle George said, as matter-of-fact as Mrs. Kovacs had been when she installed them in *her* upstairs. "Dust's not too bad, considering, is it? Everybody pitch in, and we'll have these beds made up in no time."

Making the beds was simple enough, but Rosie wondered uneasily what it was going to be like sleeping up here so far from Grandmother and Uncle George. It probably wouldn't have bothered her if she hadn't become convinced there was someone else in the house and that there were mysterious things going on that Grandmother and Uncle George refused to talk about.

Rosie's room was ready, and then the room next door, almost identical to it, was made up, too.

"All ready," Uncle George said, smiling. "We can leave that hall light on all night, in case you want the bathroom. I'll show you where that is on the way back downstairs. I wouldn't go wandering around during the night, though. This wing is safe enough, but over in the other one the fire damage was pretty bad. Your grandmother never did get it repaired, except for the roof. Had to put a new roof on or it would have rained right into the kitchen. No money to do the rest and no reason for it; she didn't use that part of the house anyway. Now, let's see about that cocoa and marshmallows, shall we?"

They paused on the way past to inspect the bathroom. It had once been a bedroom, Uncle George explained, which was why it was so large. "There wasn't any indoor plumbing when the house was built," he said. "That's why most of the pipes are where you can see them, right on the walls. There's hot water, but you have to wait a while for it to warm up. I brought up some towels earlier; they're right there in the cupboard."

Rosie decided there was no way she was going to take a bath in that huge old tub with the rust marks where the water had dripped. It stood on feet that left a space underneath where mice or maybe even rats could hide.

Not that she'd seen any sign of rodents in the house, and there was the half-grown kitten downstairs who'd probably have gone after mice if there were any. Still, it was a strange bathroom, and she didn't feel comfortable there.

It would have been a relief to go back downstairs if they hadn't all known they'd have to go up again in a little while.

Kevin went with Uncle George to the kitchen to fix the cocoa. Rosie and Nathan again sat with Grandmother in the parlor. She was knitting once more on the pink slipper, saying nothing. Rosie watched her hands, quick and clever with the needles, but with blue veins on them revealing her age.

Suddenly, breaking the silence that was absolute except for the ticking of the clock and the muted music on the radio, the telephone rang.

Rosie jumped as if she'd been poked with a pin. Even Grandmother jumped, as if she didn't hear the telephone very often.

She paused in her knitting, listening, then returned to her knit one, purl one pattern in the slipper. "George got it," she said.

A moment later, Kevin appeared in the doorway. "It's Aunt Marge," he said. "She wants to talk to Rosie."

Rosie was glad to get up and leave the room, though she didn't really want to talk to Aunt Marge. She guessed she'd be scolded, and when she reached the kitchen and picked up the telephone, she found she was right.

"Aunt Marge?" she said uncertainly.

"Rosie! Whatever possessed you to run off that way and scare everybody half to death? Mrs. Kovacs was frantic until . . . *she* called. I'd have expected Kevin to do something foolish, but you're usually so level-headed. Why did you do it?"

Rosie hadn't known anyone considered her to be level-headed. It surprised her so that for a moment she couldn't reply, until Aunt Marge repeated the question. "Why, Rosie?"

"Because"—there was a painful ache in her throat—"because we didn't want the social services people to put us into foster homes. *Different* foster homes."

There was a small silence before Aunt Marge said, "Oh. You heard us talking."

"Yes," Rosie admitted.

"But couldn't you have trusted us to work something out?"

Hope made Rosie's heart leap. "Have you?"

"Well, no, not yet, but we're trying. I mean, I talked to that Ms. Hayboldt about finding a place where they'd take all three of you. She says it's hard to find foster parents who want three kids all at once, but she's asking some of them. It's not as if it's going to be a permanent situation. Your mother will probably have to be in the hospital for another month, and then they think she'll be moved to a rest home where she can continue the physical therapy—"

Rosie interrupted without thinking. "Is Mama really going to get better? She isn't going to die?"

There was a shocked silence. "Where did you get that idea? Nobody thought she was going to die, at least not after the first couple of days. It's just that it's going to take quite a long time for her to get well enough to go back to work and take care of a family again."

"Then why did she sign papers to put us in foster

homes?'' Rosie wanted desperately to understand, to be reassured.

"Because they say it will be months before she'll be well, and there's no money to care for you until she can work again. She applied for welfare help, and they insisted they had to take charge of you until she can do it again. Rosie, you'll have to come home and we'll work it out, but you must promise never to do anything so crazy as running away again.''

Rosie said nothing. She wasn't sure she could make such a promise, though her relief that Mama was going to get better made her more optimistic.

"Rosie? Why did you go *there?* To *her?*''

Rosie glanced at Uncle George, getting out the marshmallows. Kevin was watching her, but Uncle George didn't seem to be paying any attention. She swallowed hard.

"We didn't know where else to go.''

Aunt Marge exhaled a long breath. "Hmm. Well, it's the last place I'd have thought of to go. I'm surprised she let you past the front door.''

When Rosie didn't think of any response to that, Aunt Marge pressed, "Is she treating you all right?''

Rosie thought of the mysterious face at the window, of the spooky house, of Grandmother's unfriendliness, but they'd been well fed, and offered beds.

"We're okay. As soon as their Social Security checks come, they're going to buy bus tickets to send us home.''

"She told me they'd put you on a bus. What's this about having to wait for Social Security checks?''

"They don't have the money until the checks come,'' Rosie said, hoping Uncle George wouldn't be offended by this discussion of his financial status.

"They don't have the money?" Aunt Marge echoed. She sounded disbelieving. "Why not, for heaven's sake? There used to be plenty of money! She paid Aunt Maude for taking care of us when we were kids, though I didn't know it until years later."

"She did?" Somehow that surprised Rosie; she'd thought Grandmother had simply given the girls to Aunt Maude. She wanted to tell Aunt Marge about the photos in the album, but she could hardly do that with Uncle George listening. He'd just emerged from the pantry with a box of instant cocoa. "I don't know, Aunt Marge," she said. "That's what they told us."

"Hmm. Well, it was a foolish thing to do, running off that way, and to *her,* of all people. Whatever made you think she'd want you?"

Rosie didn't think Aunt Marge meant the remark to be cruel, as if the three of them weren't worth wanting. She only meant that since Grandmother hadn't wanted *them,* her own daughters, it wasn't likely she'd have welcomed grandchildren. But it hurt. Rosie couldn't say anything.

Aunt Marge sighed. "Well, I suppose they're listening and you can't talk. You can tell me about . . . things . . . when you get home. But I had to call, to be able to tell your mother you're all right."

Alarm flared within Rosie. "Does Mama know where we are?"

"No, but I'm going to have to explain something when you don't show up to visit her tomorrow. She'd made special arrangements for you to visit, and she was so excited about it. As excited as she can get these days, anyway. I hope it doesn't upset her too much; she's so weak, she hasn't any energy to waste on disappointment."

Rosie's distress deepened. "We didn't know about the visit," she said in a small voice.

"No, and you didn't think before you took off without telling anyone where you were going, either. I expected better of you, Rosie. It was so thoughtless! Well, this is long distance, and you can't speak freely anyhow, so I'd better cut it off. I'll tell Lila you all sent your love."

"Yes," Rosie whispered, blinking against the moisture that blurred her vision.

"Good-bye, Rosie."

"Good-bye," Rosie murmured, but her aunt had already hung up.

"Here we go," Uncle George said as she replaced the receiver, "cocoa with marshmallows, coming up!"

When Rosie blinked, a little of the moisture leaked down her cheeks and she brushed it hastily away. "Aren't you and Grandmother having any?"

"No, no. We're neither of us much for sweet stuff these days. You want to carry the tray, Kevin? We'll have it in the parlor."

Rosie stared at Kevin, who was once more picking up the same clues she was.

If neither Grandmother nor Uncle George liked sweets, why did they have a carrot cake with cream cheese frosting that had had one piece cut out of it before they came, and why did they have cocoa and marshmallows—*fresh* marshmallows—in their pantry?

It didn't seem to occur to Uncle George that he was sending out conflicting information. He turned off the light in the pantry and once more locked the pantry door, dropping the key into his pocket.

Kevin suddenly rolled his eyes upward.

From overhead there had come a single muffled sound, as if something had been dropped on the floor.

Uncle George must be a bit deaf, Rosie thought, for he didn't appear to notice.

It was the person upstairs, in the east wing, who liked the sweets, Rosie thought. Who was it, and why were both her identity and her presence a deep, dark secret?

Uncle George was already out the kitchen door. Kevin paused to open the drawer that held the other flashlight, hastily crammed it into his pocket, and picked up the tray of cocoa cups again, holding it so as to shield the bulge the flashlight made.

When he entered the parlor, trailing behind the others, the bulge was gone. He'd hidden the flashlight somewhere, Rosie realized, and after Uncle George and Grandmother had gone to sleep, the three of them would use the light to investigate the mysterious east wing.

Although it was warm in the parlor, Rosie felt the goose bumps rising on her arms.

12

"REMEMBER," UNCLE GEORGE called after them, "don't wander around. It's not safe everywhere, because of the fire. But you'll be perfectly all right if you stay in the west wing."

"Okay," Kevin called back, then gave Rosie a nervous grin as they continued their climb to the second floor. The light was on again in the upstairs hallway, but now no daylight filtered through the windows.

Rosie shivered, speaking under her breath. "What did you do with the flashlight?"

"It's right here," Kevin said, patting his pocket. "We'll have to wait until they've gone to sleep, though. Grandmother's bedroom is in the main part of the house, across from the back parlor where we were tonight, and Uncle George sleeps in a little room behind the kitchen."

"How did you find that out?" Rosie asked. She hadn't heard any mention of where the others slept.

"Oh, I asked a few strategic questions," Kevin said as they moved toward their bedrooms.

Rosie stopped to look at him in alarm. "You didn't ask things that would make them realize we're planning to investigate all this mysterious stuff, did you?"

"No, of course not. Do you think I'm stupid?" He didn't wait for a reply. "I kind of like Uncle George. I think he'd let us stay, if it was up to him."

"But whatever the secret is, he knows about it," Rosie reminded him as they began to walk again.

"Yeah. But it's *her* secret, and so he won't talk about it. Somebody's living in the east wing, that's for sure. I can't figure out why it has to be a secret, though."

"What are we going to do," Nathan asked, "if we meet this mysterious person?"

Rosie was struck by a horrible thought. "What if—if she—the person—is being kept a prisoner?"

"Why would you think that?" Kevin demanded. "More likely the person is hiding. After all, they make cake and cocoa with marshmallows for her. And she sits on the porch and goes in the garden, where Rosie saw her footprints."

"What's she hiding from, then?"

"Maybe," Nathan suggested in his deliberate way, "she's a fugitive. You know, hiding out from the law. A criminal."

"We know what a fugitive is," Kevin said scathingly. "We watch TV cop shows, too. Why would Grandmother hide a criminal in her attic? Or in her burned-out upstairs?" he amended before either of them could correct him. "Well, anyway, as soon as they put out the lights downstairs . . . and we give them half an hour or so to fall asleep . . . we'll go exploring." He pulled the flashlight out and tried it. It was considerably brighter than the overhead light fixture.

The waiting was the hardest part, Rosie told herself as they huddled for the next hour in the boys' bedroom. Usually she liked ghostly tales when Kevin spun them out and tried to scare them. Tonight was different. Tonight she was too much aware of the dim lights, the shadowy places, the creaks and groans of an old house settling for the night, the branches of a tall tree scratching at the window like phantom fingers.

Finally Kevin managed to frighten even himself, she thought, because he said he'd run out of stories. He got off the bed and began to pace around the room, recounting the clues that they had and speculating on what the truth might be. Nathan contributed his own ideas.

Rosie stopped listening. Everything they guessed at sounded too far-fetched. She was getting more and more nervous as the time approached when they would leave the comparative security of this room and venture into the east wing.

Kevin ceased pacing. "I think I'm going to go look downstairs and see if they've turned off the lights there yet. We'll have to give them time to fall asleep; then we'll go."

Nathan was still sitting Indian-fashion in the middle of the bed. "I think Uncle George is hard of hearing. I doubt if he'd notice if we made any noise. He didn't seem to hear sounds right over our heads when we were in the kitchen."

"Yeah," Kevin agreed. "I think they're both kind of deaf. And I doubt if Grandmother'd come upstairs to investigate if she did hear us, because that walker doesn't fit on the stairs. But we don't want to take any chances. She'd probably wake up Uncle George to investigate if she thought we were moving around."

They sat in silence for what seemed a long time, waiting. Rosie had become so tense that she knotted her hands into fists. "What if . . . we get caught? Poking around where they told us not to go?"

"I guess they send us back to Summerville as soon as the money comes to pay for the bus tickets," Kevin said. "And they're going to do that anyway, right?"

He picked up the flashlight and let himself out into the dimly lit corridor, walking soundlessly to the top of the stairs while Rosie stood in the doorway, rubbing the goose bumps on her arms.

Kevin was back in moments, a satisfied expression on his face. "Everything's pitch black down there. I think we can go now, if we're careful. Come on."

Rosie drew in a deep breath, then had trouble letting it back out. But she was determined to learn as much as possible before they had to leave here. Maybe something they could learn would make her mother and Aunt Marge feel better about the way their mother had given them away, though so far she couldn't imagine what it would be. It had to hurt terribly to feel that your mother hadn't wanted you. Yet Grandmother had kept the snapshots of her girls as small children.

They reached the head of the stairs and continued on into new territory: the east wing of the house. It was exactly like the west wing, with doors opening on each side of the corridor. Kevin paused to open a few of them, swinging his light around inside each of the bedrooms.

At the third such inspection, he stopped dead still. Then the white beam began to move again as Rosie came to his side and peered over his shoulder, focusing her own light beyond him.

"Wow! Do you think this was *their* room? Mama's and Aunt Marge's? Look!" Kevin said.

Nathan pressed against Rosie's side, and they all stared into the bedroom.

There were twin canopied beds with dolls still propped against pillows that had nearly disintegrated with age. Toys covered in dust, so that Rosie had to stifle a sneeze, sat in neat rows in an open-fronted case, along with books whose titles they could not read.

Rosie sounded hollow. "It's like they'd just left it for a little while, except that things are . . . falling apart. And dusty."

There was even a pair of slippers sitting beside one of the beds, and dresser drawers had been left unclosed, one with a forlorn stocking hanging over its edge, as if it had been hastily emptied and no one had ever returned to put the room to rights.

It gave Rosie an eerie, sad feeling. Whether it was Mama's old room or not, some little girl had lived here once. It had been a beautiful room, years ago.

It was as if the child had left suddenly, and no one had ever come back here again.

Nathan cleared his throat. "Let's go see what's down at the end of the hall. That's where the window would be, isn't it, where Rosie saw the face?"

Very quietly, Kevin closed the door on the ghostly room, as if he, too, felt the power remaining in the faded curtains and spreads, the abandoned toys and books.

The other rooms—Kevin checked them all, now—were much the same as their own. Long unused, the beds were stripped down to mattresses with the stuffing coming out of some of them. One looked as if it had been invaded by a family of mice.

There was nothing in any of the rooms to suggest they were occupied.

Rosie busied herself trying to figure out where the window would have been and decided it was in the middle of the end of the east wing. "That one," she whispered, pointing ahead. "Right at the end of the hall. That's where I saw . . . her."

There was a ragged lace curtain there, all right. Rosie lifted it carefully, fearing it would tear at a touch, to peer outward. It was black outside; she saw nothing, yet she was certain this was the right window.

"She was standing right here," she decided, letting the curtain fall back into place. "Watching us out there in the garden."

"This is where the fire was," Nathan observed, and Kevin swung the flashlight upward so they all could see the scorch marks.

"I can smell it," Rosie said gravely. "Can't you?"

Slowly Kevin stretched out a hand to open the door on the left; it made a protesting sound as it swung inward.

Yes, this was evidently where the flames had eaten through the roof. Overhead were uncharred timbers; the roof had been replaced. The rest of the room looked pretty much the way the fire fighters must have left it when they'd finished their task.

The burned smell was very strong, and Rosie wondered how long ago the fire had occurred. The walls were blackened. Furnishings turned to charcoal stood in indistinguishable lumps. It was obvious that no one could live in that room.

There was only one door left, directly across the hallway.

Rosie held her breath, for it *must* be here that the person stayed if there was anyone upstairs at all. She waited for Kevin to open the door.

"It's locked," Kevin said. Above the beam from the flashlight, his eyes were wide and dark. "It's the only one that isn't open!"

"Maybe somebody *is* a prisoner," Nathan whispered.

Kevin lifted his free hand, hesitated, then knocked gently, so that Uncle George wouldn't hear it from downstairs.

There was only silence.

And then, as they were turning away in defeat, they heard the faint mew of a kitten.

They waited, but the sound didn't come again.

In frustration, Kevin shook the knob, and then gave a muffled exclamation. A moment later the door gave under his hand, not swinging inward like the others, but opening *outward* into the corridor.

"Got it!" Kevin cried softly, then stopped in confusion.

For behind the door that opened the wrong way was a brick wall.

The disappointment that had washed over them lingered after they'd returned to Rosie's bedroom.

"They must have walled it off because it was burned worse than the rest of the house," Kevin said, sinking onto the edge of the bed. "Maybe the floor's unsafe or something. There can't be anybody living there, Rosie."

"But I saw the face," Rosie insisted.

"And we heard a kitten behind the door. Didn't we?" Nathan asked, flopping down beside Kevin.

"We heard a kitten. I couldn't say for sure it was behind

that brick wall, though." Kevin was thoughtful. "It was hard to tell what direction it came from."

Though they talked for a while, they couldn't decide anything. All Rosie could be certain of was that she *had* seen someone watching them and that it couldn't have been either Grandmother or Uncle George, because they were in the kitchen only seconds later.

"Well," Kevin said finally, getting up, "I guess it's time to go to bed. Maybe we'll think of something else tomorrow. You're not afraid to sleep in here alone, are you, Rosie?"

She was. She'd been dreading it ever since they'd first followed Uncle George up here to make the bed. But the way Kevin said it made her reluctant to admit her fear.

"Let's both leave our doors open," she said after a moment. "Then we'll hear each other, if we need to."

"Okay," Kevin said readily. "Come on, Nate, let's go turn in."

The light was still on in the hallway, though it was so pale that when her own light was turned off Rosie's room became almost totally dark. She could hear her brothers next door, and she told herself that there was nothing to be afraid of.

She lay for a few minutes in the blackness, thinking of Mama in the hospital, Aunt Marge angry with them for running away, Mrs. Kovacs who must be disappointed in their lack of judgment, and of Grandmother and Uncle George.

She drifted into sleep, and she was not sure whether she was dreaming or had awakened when someone came into the room.

113

At first she was aware only of a shadowy form blocking out the pale light from the hall as someone stood in the doorway.

Rosie stirred with the beginning of alarm as the figure came toward her bed. "Grandmother?" she whispered.

The woman carried a flashlight; the round circle of white light slid around the walls and illuminated Rosie's face for a few moments so that she squinted against the unexpected brilliance. Then the light dropped, out of her eyes, and vaguely Rosie saw the person carrying it: a shadowy figure in some long, dark garment.

"Yes," the woman said softly. "You look so much like little Lila."

Rosie's tongue seemed thick, so that speaking was difficult. "Grandmother? Is something wrong?"

"No, no. I'm sorry I disturbed you. I thought I could just . . . look at you, without waking you. Lila . . . Lila always liked flowers, as much as I did. I thought maybe you liked them, too. I brought you some."

A faint, sweet scent wafted up as the woman placed something on the night table beside the bed. "I brought you some of my lilies. I used to let Lila pick some for her room. Go back to sleep, child. Excuse me for bothering you."

It was a dream, Rosie thought, for the woman disappeared as unexpectedly as she'd come, melting into the shadows. Somehow it didn't seem peculiar that her grandmother had come to look at her in the middle of the night. Rosie had sensed no menace in her nocturnal visitor.

She drifted off to sleep once more, waking only when she heard Nathan's voice, even more gravelly early in the morning than it usually was during the day.

"Rosie, aren't you ever going to wake up? I can smell

something good from downstairs. I think breakfast is ready."

She roused slowly from a dream about Mama fixing them pancakes and sausages on a weekend morning, a Mama who was well and happy, and they'd been planning a picnic—

Rosie sat up, wide awake. She *did* smell pancakes and sausages. "I was dreaming about food. I'm starved."

Kevin also stood at the foot of her bed, grinning. "We waited for you to wake up, but you didn't, so we thought we'd better call you."

Rosie yawned widely. "Okay. I'm getting up." She remembered, then, the *other* dream. "I thought Grandmother came in here in the middle of the night, just to look at me. She said I looked like Mama, and that Mama had always liked flowers, so she brought me some, in case I liked them, too. She smelled of some kind of flowers herself." She laughed, swinging her legs over the edge of the bed. "I can't imagine Grandmother wearing perfume, can you? Or *her* being so nice to me, acting like she really cared for Mama, after what she did to her. Why do you suppose people dream things like that?"

Kevin and Nathan had stopped smiling. Kevin, in fact, had let his mouth drop open.

"What's the matter?" Rosie demanded.

Neither of them replied, and then Rosie realized that though they were facing her, they were looking at something else.

Slowly she turned her head, and there they were on the night table, in a glass of water. Lilies of the valley, giving off the same sweet scent she remembered from her dream.

Only, of course, Rosie thought, it hadn't been a dream at all.

13

"GRANDMOTHER WAS HERE IN THE middle of the night, giving you flowers?" Kevin was incredulous.

Rosie had trouble believing it, too. It didn't seem like the Grandmother they had come to know, yet there was the evidence right in front of them: the sweet-scented lilies of the valley in a glass of water.

Nathan stared at them. "I wonder if she came and looked at us, too. She didn't leave us any flowers. Maybe she only looked at Rosie because she's so much like those pictures of Mama when she was little. Maybe she *did* like Mama once."

It was all very peculiar, Rosie thought after the boys had left and she was putting on her jeans and shirt.

On impulse, she picked up the glass of flowers when it was time to go downstairs. After all, she might not even get back up here until evening, and the flowers would be starting to wilt with no one having enjoyed them. Besides, maybe Grandmother would explain them without Rosie

116

having to bring up the subject herself if they were there on the kitchen table.

Grandmother was not in sight when they got downstairs, however. It was Uncle George, humming to himself, in the kitchen. He turned with a smile.

"Aha! I thought the smell of pancakes and sausages would roust you out of bed! It always did that to me when I was a boy! Amazing how odors can travel through a house. I've been keeping everything hot in the oven, so sit down and I'll serve it up." He looked past them when they heard the *thump, thump* of the walker. "Good morning, Dorothy. We're having a special breakfast today."

Rosie put the glass of lilies beside the syrup pitcher as she sat down, then looked toward Grandmother expectantly. She wore a plain cotton dress and the flat, sensible shoes, and her walker clumped toward them across the linoleum floor. She did not greet anyone, but eased herself into a chair, awkwardly setting aside the walker.

It must be very difficult to have to use a walker all the time, Rosie thought. She wondered if Mama would need to walk that way when she came out of the hospital; she hoped not. Mama liked to take hikes with them on Saturdays, and go roller skating sometimes. You couldn't skate if you needed a metal framework to hold you up.

"Here we go!" Uncle George said, bringing two plates to the table to slide in front of Grandmother and Rosie. "Ladies first. Blueberry syrup in the pitcher, maple syrup in the bottle."

Rosie started to reach for the maple syrup and then she saw Grandmother's face, which seemed to have gone very pale.

"Where did those come from?" she asked harshly and unexpectedly. "You mustn't pick the flowers."

Rosie followed her gaze to the little bouquet in the glass of water that she'd brought downstairs. Her throat hurt when she replied, almost whispering. "But I didn't—"

"They were on the table beside her bed when she woke up," Kevin told them.

Grandmother looked as if she were going to faint, though Rosie didn't think she was the sort of woman who fainted. One hand curled around the bar of her walker, and her knuckles were white.

Her gaze locked with Uncle George's, who also was reacting strangely. He stopped in the middle of the floor with the plates intended for the boys, as if he'd forgotten what he was doing. Rosie couldn't read his expression— alarm? warning?—as he looked into Grandmother's eyes, and then it was gone, and he was putting the plates down in front of Kevin and Nathan.

"There you are. Now mine, and we'll all eat hearty, eh?"

Had Grandmother forgotten she'd brought the flowers? Had she been walking in her sleep?

And then Rosie looked at the walker. How had Grandmother gotten upstairs, especially without making the thumping sounds that occurred when she moved along with the walker? Could she have walked in her sleep, without remembering this morning?

Not without the walker, Rosie thought numbly. And the figure that had loomed over her had not been using a walker. She had carried a flashlight in one hand and the glass of lilies in the other. She couldn't have done that while hanging on to the bars of a walker.

118

Kevin was clearly as bewildered as she was, though when Uncle George began to eat, Kevin did, too. The silence was uncomfortable, but after a moment or two each of the others picked up their forks and cut into their pancakes. Only Nathan seemed unaware of the tension, or at least unaware of the reason for it.

The little bouquet intruded on Rosie's thoughts, so that she wasn't as hungry as she'd been a few minutes earlier. It looked so innocent, so pretty, but what did it mean? Why was Grandmother so upset by the flowers? And if *she* hadn't brought them, who was the person who had?

Grandmother didn't have much appetite, either. In fact, while Rosie gradually regained hers and finally did justice to Uncle George's special breakfast, Grandmother scarcely touched her food.

Uncle George was cheerful as he picked up the plates after they'd finished. "Well, looks like kitty's going to get your leftovers, Dorothy," he commented as he carried Grandmother's almost untouched breakfast over to the counter. "Where are you, Ophelia?"

"Ophelia?" Nathan echoed. "Who's Ophelia?"

"That consarned kitten that's usually underfoot," Uncle George said. "Here, kitty, kitty!"

"We heard a cat last night, upstairs," Nathan told him.

"Upstairs? Oh, well, I'd better go up and take a look. See if she's gotten herself locked in somewhere," Uncle George said after a moment. "I expect there are a few mice up there, tempting her. And maybe the wind blew a door shut on her or something."

But there were no windows open, Rosie protested silently—nowhere for a wind to come in. And the kitten had sounded as if it were behind that bricked-up doorway, though that seemed impossible since the bricks had obviously been there for a long time.

Her head was beginning to ache, trying to figure out all the odd things about this place.

If only she weren't so worried about being separated from her brothers and going into a foster home, Rosie thought, it would be a relief to return to Summerville.

"I'll help you look for the kitten," Nathan offered, but Uncle George waved him aside.

"No, no, she won't be hard to find."

"What kind of a name is Ophelia?" Nathan persisted, unwilling to let the subject go.

"Ophelia was the name of a character in a famous play," Uncle George told him. "Tell you what, you kids go out and play, why don't you? Have a good time."

"Sure," Kevin agreed. "It was a great breakfast, Uncle George."

Once outside, however, Kevin echoed the things Rosie had been thinking. "This place gives me the creeps. What the heck's going on? Grandmother brings you flowers when you're asleep, then bawls you out for picking them. What difference would it have made if you *had* picked them? And who's kidding who about that cat? I've been thinking about that walled-up room." He looked upward, as if he might be able to see through the walls. "Right there, it would be, right, Rosie? The room to the left of the window where you saw the face at the end of the hallway? If the cat's in there, there has to be a way in."

They decided to walk around the farm, or what remained of it—parts of it had been sold off years earlier, Uncle

George had told them—and on the way Rosie paused again to look at the flower bed.

Then she gave a startled exclamation and stooped to look more closely.

"What's the matter?" Nathan asked.

"There's another footprint. A heel print, I mean. See? Someone wearing a high heel, and it was made since we were here yesterday, because this is over the top of the earlier ones; it's sharper."

"It wasn't Uncle George," Kevin said. "And it wasn't Grandmother, either. Even if she put on high heels to come out here and pick flowers, there'd be the marks of her walker beside the marks from her shoes. So Rosie's right. There *has* to be someone else here."

His eyes were suddenly bright. "Maybe it wasn't Grandmother who brought you the flowers, Rosie. Maybe it was this other person."

Rosie was aware of the morning sun warm on her back, of the stillness except for the twitter of an unseen bird in one of the nearby trees, and the beat of her own heart.

"It looked like Grandmother," she said. "But she didn't have a walker."

"Who is she, then?" Nathan wanted to know.

There was no answer for that. Not yet.

"We'll have to keep trying to figure it out," Kevin said, and Rosie was torn between a similar determination and a desire to forget it all and go home, where things were familiar rather than mysterious and frightening. Except, of course, that now the situation at home was frightening, too.

They walked past the old barn, too empty to be worth exploring again, and found the remains of what appeared to have been a chicken house, for there was a fenced yard next to a jumble of burned timbers.

"Another fire," Kevin observed, kicking at one of the blackened supports, which came down with a crash when he pushed at it. "In the house, and now this one. I guess they're too far from the fire station for the fire department to get here quickly. They come so fast when there's a fire in town. I never thought about what it would be like living out in the country. It's kind of scary to think about it."

They wandered on over a small hill to where a stream cut through the property. It had once been pasture, they guessed, but now it was overgrown with grass and clover, sweet-scented in the summer air.

None of them could forget, however, what had happened at the house, and as soon as they reached a fence that marked a boundary of the farm, they turned back. Clouds moved overhead, shutting out the sun, and the temperature dropped enough so that Rosie wished she had a sweater.

Nathan had stopped and was looking backward. "I think I dropped my pen. I had it in my pocket, and it's not there. The one that used to be Daddy's."

"Well, go back and look around. Maybe you even lost it yesterday. You rolled in the hay in the barn," Kevin said. "It probably fell out then."

Nathan hesitated. "Will you help me look?"

"If you can't find it right away, I suppose so." If it hadn't been a special pen, one of the last things Daddy had given Nathan, Rosie was sure Kevin would have told him to forget it.

Nathan trotted off, leaving them standing there. After a moment they began to walk toward the house.

"We need to look around in the east wing again," Kevin decided. "How are we going to do it without them knowing what we're up to?"

They didn't have time to ponder that for long, because when they reached the veranda, they were met by Uncle George, looking less cheerful than usual.

"Something wrong?" Kevin guessed, pausing on the top step.

"Your grandmother's having chest pains. The doctor thinks we should take her in to his office right away. It's probably not another heart attack, but he doesn't think we should take a chance. I'll bring the car around to this door, and we can leave in just a minute."

"You don't need to worry about us," Kevin said quickly. "We'll be all right on our own. We'll take a walk beyond the creek and see if the blackberries are getting ripe over there on the edge of the woods."

"It's a bit early for blackberries," Uncle George said, but it was clear his mind wasn't on berries. "You might get a few, I suppose, but don't pick any unless they're fully ripe. If they're too sour, they aren't much use."

"No." They looked up to see Grandmother in the doorway, her skin drawn taut over her cheekbones and looking almost gray. "They can't stay here. They can pick berries some other time." She spoke with an effort, as if breathing was difficult. "Get in the car."

"We can't go without Nathan," Rosie said. And then, for once in her life thinking quickly, she added, "He wandered off somewhere. We'll have to go find him."

Uncle George took a good look at Grandmother. "Is the pain worse, Dorothy?"

Her lips had a bluish tinge and they moved stiffly. "It's . . . bad enough."

"We can't wait, then. The kids'll be all right, they'll be out in the field. Nothing to worry about. If they check you into the hospital after all, I'll come right back. Come on, I'll help you down the steps and I'll get the car."

Perhaps Grandmother would have resisted further, but it was obvious she was in pain. She let him assist her off the porch and stood breathing in short gasps.

Even though she was alarmed at the way Grandmother looked, excitement bubbled up through Rosie; they were going to be left on their own for an hour or two, and in daylight! "Maybe we'd better take the pails, in case there are berries ready to pick," she said, before she lost her courage.

"Oh, yes." Uncle George paused and dug out the key. "They're in the pantry, you know where. Don't forget to relock it."

A few minutes later the old sedan was easing out of the driveway with Uncle George behind the wheel and Grandmother, decidedly unwell, beside him.

Rosie hoped she was going to be all right, but there was nothing they could do about that. The important thing was that Grandmother and Uncle George were gone.

"Let's go," Kevin said tensely. "Let's find out as much as we can before they come back."

"Not without Nathan," Rosie said, hesitating, and then she saw him coming from the direction of the barn, waving the pen.

"I found it!" he called, trotting toward them. "Where did Grandmother and Uncle George go?"

"To the doctor's in town," Kevin said. "Grandmother isn't feeling well. We've got the house to ourselves, so let's see what we can find out."

Nathan's hand stretched out to Rosie's and she squeezed it as they went into the house together.

14

"WE'LL GET THE PAILS OUT," KEVIN said, moving directly to the pantry door and inserting the key in the lock, "so it will look as if we went to pick berries. Then we'll just say they weren't really ripe. *That's* true enough; I tasted one this morning and it was pretty sour."

Rosie was shivering with either excitement or fear; she wasn't sure which. "How long do you suppose they'll be gone?"

"Long enough, I'll bet, if we hurry," Kevin assured her. He set aside a box of kitchen matches and one of tea to reach the plastic buckets they'd been given before for berry picking; then, moving out, he put the yellow plastic pails on the counter beside the sink and slid the key into his pocket. "Come on, let's do a quick pass through the downstairs rooms, in case there's a clue down here. Maybe whoever else is here just escaped from a first-floor room and wandered upstairs to where Rosie saw her looking out the window."

"You don't really think Grandmother's holding someone prisoner, do you?" It wasn't the first time they'd talked about that, but the idea was still shocking to Rosie.

Kevin had led the way out into the main hallway and was opening doors opposite the kitchen. "Grandmother's strange enough so I guess I'd believe anything. Wow, look at this junk! What's that thing?"

"It's a form you fit dresses onto," Rosie said, with a glance at the shadowy shape in the darkened room full of old furniture and odds and ends. "I saw one on TV once. What about Uncle George? Would you believe *he'd* lock anybody up?"

"Who knows? He seems nice, but maybe it's only a put-on, to make us think he's okay. This is his room over here."

Rosie felt uncomfortable opening the door to someone else's room. Mama had taught them to respect other people's privacy. Yet it seemed important to learn what was going on here, and they'd never have a better opportunity than right now.

Uncle George's room was small and neat. The bed was made up with a blue spread; there were slippers beside it, and a small table held a reading light, several books, and a pair of glasses. A dresser and a straight chair completed the furnishings.

"No clues here," Rosie said, sounding rather out of breath.

They moved rapidly through the ground floor of the big house, opening each door, glancing around enough to assure themselves that no third party used it.

Some of the rooms had no furniture whatever. Those that did included a study that looked as if it hadn't been entered in years, and Grandmother's bedroom.

There was no mistaking that. It was tidy and rather

homey in an old-fashioned way, with a cheerful patchwork quilt on the bed, a cushioned rocking chair, and a wall of shelves that held books and curios, everything from seashells to an old corncob pipe.

And there were more photographs.

Nathan stepped over the threshold, staring at the pictures on the dresser. "That looks like Aunt Marge, only she's too young."

Rosie followed him with a few tentative steps. This really was an invasion of privacy, yet she couldn't help herself. She had to know more about Grandmother; she wanted to understand why her own mother had been given away when she was younger than Nathan was now, why Grandmother hadn't wanted her.

As far as Rosie knew, there had never been any letters or gifts exchanged between Grandmother and Mama or Aunt Marge after they'd been sent to live with Aunt Maude. She had taken it for granted, from what she'd heard Mama say, that Grandmother simply hadn't wanted her two little daughters.

Then why, Rosie wondered now, did Grandmother have framed photographs of both of them sitting on her dresser as well as their school pictures in her albums?

"It's Mama's graduation picture," Rosie said slowly. "When she graduated from high school. And the other one is Aunt Marge's; Mama's got one like it. Where did she get them? She didn't have anything to do with them when they were in school."

Kevin hadn't bothered to come into the room. "Probably Aunt Maude sent them to her; she's the one who paid for the pictures, I guess. Come on, we don't have any time to waste. We've got to find whoever's living in this house."

"And rescue the kitten," Nathan said unexpectedly. "I don't think Uncle George found it, because Grandmother got sick."

It was a little easier to explore in daylight, but not much less spooky, Rosie thought, as they climbed the stairs and began to make their way along the corridor into the east wing. It was getting darker outside. If the predicted rain came, it would give them an excuse for not having picked any berries. She hoped there wouldn't be a major storm. It was already gloomy inside the house, and if it got any darker it would be nearly as eerie as it was at night.

"This time we'll open every single door," Kevin instructed, flinging one open in demonstration. "Holler if you find one that looks like anybody's been in it lately. Or if you hear the kitten," he added, poking his head in to give a cursory examination to the next room in the row.

But room after room sat empty and dusty. The corners were deep with shadows, and they jumped when there was a rumble of thunder. A moment later the lightning came in a blazing, jagged streak, visible through the window at the end of the hall, followed by another roll of thunder.

"Close," Kevin commented. "Boy, maybe I'd better go back to our room and get the flashlight. I didn't think we'd need it. You guys keep looking, and I'll catch up to you in a minute, okay?"

Rain suddenly slashed at the windows, and they could hear it on the roof, a real downpour.

Rosie swallowed. She wasn't afraid of storms, not usually, but in this house it seemed different.

It didn't bother Nathan, however. He was opening yet

another door, peering inside, reclosing it. "Here, kitty, kitty," he coaxed.

And then, just before another crash of thunder, they heard it: a faint but distinct mewing.

Nathan's face was a pale oval, except for the dark rims of his glasses, in what had become a near-twilight dimness. "Which direction did it come from?"

The storm was in full fury now. Rain slashed audibly at the windows and over their heads on the roof. It made Rosie feel disoriented, caught between reality and illusion. She hoped Kevin would hurry back as yet another crack of lightning showed momentarily through the window.

It was as though the storm sucked the oxygen out of the air, leaving less than she needed to breathe. Rosie took a great gulping breath; she mustn't let herself be panicked because of a stupid old thunder and lightning storm.

Nathan was waiting for her answer, and Rosie made herself calm down. "I think it was back there, where we heard it before. If it's somehow gotten into that walled-off room, though, I don't see how we're going to rescue it."

"If it's in that back room," Nathan reasoned, "it didn't get in through the brick wall. There must be another way in. Let's try the room next to it. We didn't really look around in there before."

He moved ahead of her into a room that seemed as deserted as all the others, a bedroom that hadn't been occupied for many years. They hadn't been checking closets, but there was one here, on the wall this chamber shared with the one that was closed off, and Nathan jerked the door open.

Rosie was right behind him, and for a moment she

thought she was finding out what it was like to have a heart attack.

For long seconds her heart seemed to stop beating, and then it began to pound so loudly that she felt deafened.

Beyond the door, moving toward them from her own side of the empty closet space, was the figure who had brought the flowers to her room last night.

Not Grandmother, Rosie thought, feeling numb. The woman stepped backward, as startled as they were, and the light from a lamp inside the farther room fell upon her face.

Not Grandmother, but looking like Grandmother.

Rosie stared with her mouth open. Nathan backed up until he ran into her and stopped, and her arms went around him automatically for a few seconds, then dropped to her sides.

"Lila? No, Lila's daughter," the woman said, and even the voice was a great deal like Grandmother's.

Rosie felt as if her lips had been frozen. They didn't want to move.

"Come in," the woman said, and stepped backward just as Kevin reappeared behind the others.

Kevin's jaw had gone slack, too. "Who are you?" he blurted.

The woman smiled. She was not as tall as she had seemed when she stood beside Rosie's bed, not as tall as Grandmother was. The similarity between them, however, was uncanny.

The features were almost identical, and all at the same time this woman seemed to be both older and younger than Grandmother. Her hair was unstreaked by gray, and it was beautifully done, swept back and up in a way that looked young, but out-of-date, the way women wore their hair in old, old movies. Under a dark velvet cloak she was wearing a long dress in a deep shade of red and a necklace of what appeared to be rubies and diamonds, which glittered in the lamplight. More jewels twinkled in her ears.

She looked, Rosie thought, dazed, as if she were about to set off for a formal party, complete with makeup.

As astonishing as this woman was, the room into which she led them was almost more so.

The rest of the house might be shabby and out-of-date, with only a few rooms still comfortable and livable. This area, a combination bed-sitting room, overflowed with personal mementos, pictures, clutter, and color. Bright fabrics, mirrors everywhere, soft chairs, a small piano, and a television set made it hard to believe the inhabitant could be a prisoner here. Besides, she hadn't been locked in.

"Come in," the woman said. She bent to scoop up the kitten that rubbed against her ankles, cuddling it close to her face, smiling. "Poor Ophelia, she hasn't had her breakfast yet, and neither have I. George must have forgotten me. Or have you come to bring it?"

Rosie made her lips move. "No. We . . . didn't know you were here."

"Who—who are you?" Kevin croaked, sounding nearly as husky as Nathan usually did.

The woman smiled, stroking the kitten. "Why, I'm Ellen, of course. Ellen Waxwell."

Rosie stiffened. Prickles ran along her spine and up into her hair.

Unable to speak, she stood looking into the unknown yet eerily familiar face, feeling as if all her blood were draining out the soles of her feet.

"I'm Dorothy's sister," the woman said. "I'm your aunt Ellen."

How could that be? Ellen Waxwell was dead, Rosie thought; she had died in a fire many years ago. They had seen her headstone in the graveyard out there in the tangled woods.

Overhead, thunder rolled and crashed, and in the seconds after the light went out, plunging all their faces into shadows, lightning again split the sky beyond the windows.

A nightmare, Rosie thought desperately, she was caught in the grip of a nightmare, and any moment now she would wake up and everything would be fine.

The woman who said she was Ellen Waxwell suddenly thrust the kitten away, her mood changing. "Naughty Ophelia! You've snagged my dress!"

Automatically, Rosie put out her arms to accept the cat. It was warm and soft against her, and she knew that it was real. This was actually happening.

She wasn't going to wake up and discover that everything was fine at all.

15

"SIT DOWN, SIT DOWN!" SAID THE woman who called herself Ellen Waxwell. She swept some sort of filmy garment off a chair and picked up a sheaf of typewritten pages from the sofa to put them atop some of the books on a low table. "I'm studying a script," she said, when Rosie's gaze followed her actions. "I'm an actress, you know. Don't worry about the lights, we can see well enough until George changes the fuse."

By this time Rosie was totally bewildered. As she told her brothers later, she wondered if she'd fallen, like Alice, down the rabbit hole. Any minute now she might encounter the White Rabbit, babbling about being late.

Nathan cleared his throat. "Uncle George isn't here. He took Grandmother to the doctor's."

"Besides," Kevin added, "I don't think it's a fuse. I think the storm took out the power."

"Oh. Well, sit down, anyway. Would you like some cookies and tea?"

After a moment, during which the only thing to be heard

was the storm that raged around the house, Kevin said, "No, thank you."

"No, thank you," Nathan and Rosie echoed.

It was not really dark, for it was, after all, only the middle of the morning. Rosie, glancing around the big room, saw her own pale face reflected and re-reflected dozens of times in the mirrors that were everywhere.

There was a huge poster on one wall, of a beautiful young woman theatrically posed, and after a few moments Rosie realized that it was probably of this woman, many years ago.

Ellen Waxwell *had* been an actress, but how could this be the same person?

Rosie was confused and uneasy, perched on the edge of a chair that looked more comfortable than it was. The woman wasn't a ghost, or she wouldn't have helped herself to a cookie from a plate on the low table.

"I love cookies," Ellen said. "Sweets of any kind, actually. I guess they aren't good for me. That's what Dorothy says. She only lets me have a little each day. For my own good. I have to be careful what I eat, of course. One has to keep one's figure when one is on the stage."

She was the one who craved the carrot cake, and the cocoa and marshmallows, as well as the cookies, Rosie thought. But why was it such a secret? Why had Grandmother and Uncle George kept this woman away from them? *Why had they said she was dead?*

She had brought the flowers during the night, however.

Rosie had trouble finding her voice, but she felt she had to speak. "Thank you for the bouquet," she said, and was chagrined to find that her voice squeaked.

Ellen smiled. "Oh, you found them. I thought you might

like them. Lila always did. She used to help me work in the garden when she was small. Did you know I named your mother? I wanted to call her Lily, for my favorite flowers. Dorothy wouldn't let me do that, but Lila was close." Ellen helped herself to another cookie.

The thunder and lightning seemed to have passed. Already the sky was growing lighter, though rain still streaked the windows. Rosie thought that Nathan and Kevin were as puzzled and uncomfortable as she was.

"I'm glad you came to see me," Ellen said. The kitten had now crawled into her lap and she stroked it absently, having forgotten that it had earned her displeasure only a short time before. "I get so lonesome sometimes, but Dorothy says nobody must know I'm here. I never get to go anywhere, except to the doctor in Kansas City."

"How come you go all that way?" Nathan asked. He had changed his mind about the cookie and reached out to take one. "There must be a doctor closer than that, like the one Grandmother went to."

"Oh, Dorothy's gone to Dr. Fallows for years. But I can't go to him. I need the specialist, Dr. Milikan, in Kansas City. And, of course, Dr. Fallows thinks I'm dead."

Rosie's sense of unreality increased to the point that it began to make her head ache. She spoke very carefully. "You have a grave out in the little cemetery."

Ellen nodded and poured herself tea from a fancy pot. "Yes. It's a nice tombstone, isn't it?"

This had to be the most peculiar conversation Rosie had ever heard, let alone participated in. "Why do you have a tombstone, if you're still alive?"

A look of consternation passed over Ellen's features.

"I'm not supposed to talk about that, not even to Dr. Milikan. She would probably turn me in if she knew about me, Dorothy says. Dorothy gets very cross if I talk to anyone. She scolds me. Sometimes, if she's very angry, she doesn't let me have my cake."

This wasn't getting any clearer, and Rosie was aware of the passing of time. Grandmother and Uncle George might be home any minute, and there was now more mystery than ever, except that they'd found this woman who lived hidden away upstairs.

It was easy, though, to imagine how unpleasant it would be to have Grandmother angry at you. "Turn you in where?" Rosie asked, swallowing hard.

"To the authorities. You know, the police. I made her promise that she wouldn't ever let them lock me up again. I would do *anything* to keep from being locked up again." Ellen had a wild, determined expression that almost discouraged further questions. Only they might never have another chance to find out what was going on here, and Rosie didn't see how they could simply go home to Summerville without knowing more than they did right now. There were more unanswered questions than ever.

It was an effort to form the words because her lips were so stiff. "Why would the police want to lock you up?"

"Because of the . . . you know." Ellen sipped at her tea. "It was terrible, when they locked me up before. I ran away and hid, first in the barn and then out in the . . ." A canny expression crossed her face, and she didn't finish her sentence. "Anyway, I got hungry and had to come back to the house for something to eat, and they caught me. Dorothy let them take me."

137

"They put you in jail?" Nathan asked, shocked. "What did you do?"

"Not in jail," Ellen corrected. "In that . . . place. Some of the people in there were crazy. Mentally ill," she amended, as if she were a child who had been reprimanded for using the wrong term.

Mentally ill. The words rang in Rosie's head, bringing understanding of a sort, and also alarm. Was Aunt Ellen mentally ill? That still wouldn't explain why the others said she was *dead.*

"I hated it there!" Ellen said petulantly. Her moods changed so rapidly that it was hard to keep up. "The food was awful. We never had good desserts, only yucky puddings and stewed fruit. And they only let me take a few of my lovely clothes. . . ." Her fingers stroked the rich red fabric of her gown. "At least here I have my own things around me. Dorothy promised I'd never have to go back there, but she says I have to stay here, away from people. No one can know I'm here. And I'm sick, you know. I suppose I'll die before Dorothy does. I'm ten years older, and I'm sick. She's been very good to me, she *has.*"

This last was said very earnestly, as if someone had challenged this; Ellen leaned toward Rosie, who was the closest to her.

"I know it was hard on her, to give up Lila and Marge, but she had to take care of me, you see. You understand that, don't you? She didn't *want* to send the girls to live with Maude. That's why she sometimes gets so angry with me, because it's my fault she had to give them up. Maude sends her pictures sometimes, did you know that?"

Rosie felt as if her head were spinning; she had to get this straight. "Mama and Aunt Marge were sent to Aunt Maude because Grandmother had to take care of you? But that was so many years ago! Were you sick then, too?"

This time Ellen's expression turned sly. "Well, you know. I had that . . . problem. But it's all worked out fine."

Fine? Rosie wanted to shout. *Fine that my mother and Aunt Marge were sent away from home and never told why? Fine that to this day they are hurt and bitter about it? That they think their mother hates them? Didn't want them?*

Rosie was suffocating. The storm was dying away; there was even a rainbow appearing through the window. But she felt as if the storm still battered her, bruising her flesh.

She no longer doubted that this woman *was* Ellen Waxwell. She looked so much like Grandmother that they had to be sisters. But she didn't understand any of the rest of it, and it was important that she understand.

It was painful to her that Mama had signed papers turning them over to someone else, but she understood that it was because she was very ill and that she wouldn't be able to care for the three of them for quite a while yet. But Mama had never known why *she* had been given away; she still suffered from the abandonment. If there was a reason why it had happened, wouldn't it help Mama to know what it was? Might it even help her to get better?

"Dorothy said it would be all right if I stayed here and behaved myself. One of these days I'm going to be on the stage again. I look at scripts all the time—George gets them for me, bless him—but I haven't found the right one yet."

Rosie's stomach had tightened into a sick knot. It had to be a delusion on Ellen's part, that she was going to be an actress again. She was dressed and made up and had her hair styled like a young woman, but she was old; ten years older than Grandmother. In this light her face seemed young, but her hands gave her away. They were veined and old, like Aunt Maude's.

What had Ellen done that they had put her in an institution with people who were mentally ill? And most important of all, *did she belong in one now?*

Kevin was twisting a button on his shirt, watching Ellen in a sort of horrified fascination. "If you were locked up in that . . . place, did they let you out? Or did you"—his Adam's apple bobbed as he swallowed"—get out somehow?"

Ellen laughed, and in a way it was a magical sound: tinkling, silvery, melodic. But it gave Rosie chills up her spine, because Ellen was not a fairy child, like the laughter. She was an old woman, a very peculiar old woman.

"I was more clever than they thought. I waited until a Sunday afternoon, when all the visitors were there, and I borrowed some clothes"—the way she said it made Rosie guess that she really meant she'd stolen them—"and simply walked out the front gate with a woman who thought I was another visitor. I'd taken off all my makeup, so I'd look plain, and the guard didn't even recognize me. They didn't miss me for hours, and by that time I'd gotten a ride with a very nice gentleman who not only took me into town but lent me the money for bus fare."

"So you came back here." Kevin sounded as hollow as Rosie felt.

"Yes. This is where Dorothy was, after all. And then there was the fire, of course, and when they found Sylvia's body, they thought it was mine, so they didn't look for me any longer."

A body? Rosie sucked for air, panicky now. She wanted to throw open the window; in fact, she went so far as to push herself out of the chair, unable to sit there any longer. "It's so close in here—" she murmured, and Ellen immediately rose from her own seat.

"I'll open a window; it is close. There, that's nice, isn't it? The air always smells so clean and fresh after a storm. Look, see the rainbow!"

Nobody paid any attention to the rainbow. A body, Rosie thought. Had Ellen killed someone named Sylvia? Was Aunt Ellen a murderer?

She heard the sound of a car and glanced down into the backyard where the old sedan came into view.

They were home, Grandmother and Uncle George.

No doubt she and the boys would be severely scolded, maybe even punished, for coming up here and finding Aunt Ellen, Rosie thought. But she didn't know whether to be afraid of them or glad they were home.

She didn't want to be here any longer with Ellen Waxwell, who had escaped from a mental institution and might have killed someone named Sylvia.

She saw from Kevin's face that he, too, was afraid.

"They're home," Rosie said. "Grandmother's getting out of the car. She must be better."

Beside her, Ellen twisted her hands together. "They're going to be angry with me," she said, and Rosie saw that she, too, was apprehensive, expecting to be punished. "Maybe you'd better go, before they find out you've been talking to me. Dorothy will be furious with me. They told me to stay away from you, that you'd be gone in a few days, but when I heard you were Lila's children, I couldn't resist taking a look. . . . I loved Lila so, when she was a little girl. You *do* look like her."

She turned to Rosie, lifting a hand to touch her cheek,

and Rosie jerked backward. The thought of being touched by that gnarled old hand with the long red fingernails sent her fleeing, feet pounding on the bare wood floors in her haste to get away. She heard Nathan and Kevin behind her, heard Aunt Ellen call something after them, heard the door closing downstairs as Grandmother and Uncle George entered the house.

They were home, but something dark and horrid was going on in this house, and Rosie didn't feel safe at all. She stopped when she reached the bottom of the stairs and looked around. Like Ellen, she wanted a place to hide.

There was nowhere Grandmother wouldn't find them, she thought in despair. She waited, trembling, for whatever was going to happen next.

16

UNCLE GEORGE'S VOICE SOUNDED the same as ever: friendly and nonthreatening. "Oh, good, there you are. Got inside before the storm broke, I see. That was quite a show old Mother Nature put on, wasn't it? Turn on the light there in the parlor, will you, Kevin? Your grandmother is all right, but she needs to sit and rest a bit. Just the stress kicking up her angina again; she has some medicine for it."

Rosie stood rooted at the foot of the stairs, unable to move or speak. Kevin, however, was recovering more quickly. "The electricity's off," he said.

"Oh? Well, that means we can't heat water for tea, either. They usually get the crews out very quickly, though. Give it a try; see if by any chance they've repaired whatever it was."

He came toward them in the dimness of the hallway, with Grandmother's walker making its muffled *thump, thump* as she followed along behind.

Aunt Ellen's words still rang in Rosie's ears. *Dorothy will*

143

be furious with me. They told me to stay away from you. . . .

"Dorothy was so looking forward to a nice cup of hot tea," Uncle George said, disappointed. "I was, myself."

Kevin had reached the parlor and the light switch. "Hey, it's back on!"

"Good, good. Come on, Dorothy," Uncle George said to Grandmother. "We'll get you settled here, and maybe Rosie can run and put on a kettle of water for that tea, eh, young lady?"

Grandmother went past Rosie and Nathan where they stood watching without ever looking at them. Perhaps it was only the way the light filtered through the closing-in trees that made her look older and gave her skin a faint greenish cast.

"That's it," Uncle George approved as Kevin turned on another lamp next to Grandmother's chair. "The storm cooled off the air, didn't it? Fetch the afghan from the sofa there to put across her lap, eh?"

Once the others had entered the parlor, Rosie made her legs work. She practically ran down the hallway toward the kitchen.

Her first thought was not to put on the water, however, for the tea. It was to call for help.

Not the local police. For all she knew, the chief in that little town might be Uncle George's good friend, who wouldn't believe a word Rosie said. No, it had to be someone she could trust. If only Mama were home, she thought, but of course if Mama weren't in the hospital, they wouldn't have come here in the first place.

Aunt Marge, then. Aunt Marge was angry with them for having run away, but she wouldn't want anything to happen

To Grandmother's House We Go

to them. Rosie had called Aunt Marge at work before, when Mama had her stroke and then afterward from Mrs. Kovacs' house, and she remembered the number.

So far nobody had followed her. Nathan had apparently gone into the parlor, too. Rosie's fingers shook when she reached for the telephone and began to dial. No, she thought, she'd forgotten the area code; they were in a different state, so she must first dial a *one* and then *two-one-seven* for the area code, then the number where Aunt Marge worked. Rosie prayed that Uncle George would stay in the parlor.

"Marjorie Woodruff, please," she said when the receptionist answered, and a moment later her aunt was on the line.

"Aunt Marge, could you come and get us?" Rosie blurted. "Instead of our waiting until they can buy us bus tickets?"

Aunt Marge's voice was sharp. "Come and get you? Whatever for? Rosie, has something happened?"

Rosie's mind was whirling. How could she explain, in only a few minutes over the phone, why she was so frightened? Did Aunt Marge know about Aunt Ellen, that she was kept a prisoner in the house, or at least hidden away from everyone?

"You . . . you know about Aunt Ellen," she said tentatively, and heard Aunt Marge's impatience.

"Ellen? She died years ago, in a fire. What does she have to do with anything? Rosie, I *can't* come after you. I have to accompany my boss to a convention in Chicago Friday and Saturday, and it's much too far to drive to Missouri and back in the one day I have off, on Sunday. Besides that, if

I came after you, I'd have to see *her.* I hadn't spoken a word to her in twenty-seven years until she called me about you the other day, and I've no interest in talking to her again."

The bitterness was so strong, shutting out any other consideration, that Rosie felt scalded by it. She tried to think of persuading words, but in the background another phone rang, and Aunt Marge said with crisp finality, "You'll have to come on the bus, Rosie. I have another call coming in, I have to go."

And the line was dead.

Suddenly aware of approaching voices and footsteps, Rosie turned on the burner under the kettle and reached for the canister of tea on the back of the counter. She had the cups down by the time the others reached the kitchen.

Her heart was hammering and her eyes stung. She'd tried, but she hadn't been clever enough to say the right words that would have brought help.

What would Grandmother do if she knew they had discovered her sister living upstairs?

"Anyone else for tea? Or cocoa?" Uncle George wanted to know as he followed Kevin into the room. "No? Ah, didn't get to the berries before the rain came, eh? Well, they probably weren't really sweet yet, anyway. It's a bit early for wild blackberries."

Rosie listened to them, catching Kevin's gaze when Uncle George finally poured the tea into two cups and put them on a tray.

"Come along, we'll sit with your grandmother while she has her tea. Then I shouldn't wonder if she'd like to lie down for a time; it's tiring to hurt, I'll tell you, though she's feeling much better now."

When they were once more uneasily seated in the parlor,

Rosie didn't think Grandmother looked better. She looked old and tired. And frightening? Rosie wasn't sure whether Grandmother was someone to be afraid of or not.

Uncle George was in a chatty mood. He started reminiscing about the old days when he and Albert, Mama's father, had been boys in this house. Some of the stories he told, like the one about when they had attempted to put on a circus using the farm animals and the goat had knocked down the prop for the clothesline and dragged their mother's laundry through the chicken yard, might have made them all laugh under other circumstances.

Rosie was beyond being amused by anything. She kept remembering that room upstairs with all the mirrors and the clutter and Aunt Ellen with her old hands and young-old face with too much makeup, and the headstone in the little graveyard.

If Aunt Ellen wasn't buried under her own headstone, Rosie wondered, who was?

Rosie was the only one facing the doorway, and so she was the only one who saw the figure flit past it, silent, holding a warning finger to heavily rouged lips.

Aunt Ellen in her long scarlet gown, a secretive smile turning up the corners of her mouth, met Rosie's gaze for long seconds, then vanished toward the back of the house.

Rosie heard the ticking of the clock, Uncle George's voice (though the words themselves didn't register), and the faint *creak, creak* of the rocker as Grandmother kept it going.

She strained to hear any sounds Aunt Ellen might make, but there was nothing. Until, perhaps, the faint sound of the closing of a door?

Uncle George stood up, placing his cup on the tray and then reaching for Grandmother's cup. "Finished? You want any help getting to bed for a nap, Dorothy?"

Grandmother stopped rocking. "I'm feeling better. We'd ought to be thinking about what to have for lunch, I suppose. And maybe you'd better . . . tend to your . . . chores."

There was that word again. *Chores.* To Rosie it had always meant things like carrying out the garbage, or if you lived on a farm, milking the cows and feeding the chickens. Yet there were no cows or chickens here, and Kevin had carried out the garbage earlier that morning.

Besides, there was something in the way that Grandmother spoke, hesitating between the words, that altered their meaning.

She meant, Rosie thought, something to do with Aunt Ellen, locked into that room upstairs. Only, of course, Aunt Ellen was no longer there.

"Lunch," Uncle George echoed, picking up the tray to return the cups to the kitchen. "Well, let's see. There's cold roast, will that do for sandwiches? And I'll get out some canned peaches, how will that be?"

Rosie stood up with the others as they began to move toward the back of the house. She felt suffocated again, with the effort of breathing; would Aunt Ellen surprise them when they walked into the kitchen? Had she come down to help herself to more cookies or some of the carrot cake, when no one was around to stop her?

The kitchen was empty when they reached it, but before Rosie had time to feel relief, Uncle George cried out and slammed the tray down on the counter beside the sink, so hard that one of the cups actually jumped off from it.

Only then did it register in Rosie's consciousness that the pantry door stood wide open.

"The key!" Uncle George demanded, turning to Kevin. "You didn't relock the pantry!"

Kevin, after a moment of being too startled to react, reached into his pocket. "I'm sorry. I forgot. We were going to put the berry pails back—"

Uncle George looked into the pantry, reached up to the shelf where they had found the pails, and emerged looking so alarmed that Rosie was frightened, too, even before she knew what was wrong.

Uncle George's voice was hoarse as he spoke to Grandmother, who had just gotten through the doorway.

"The matches are gone. She's taken the matches."

For a moment Grandmother swayed a little, even as she clung to the bars of the walker.

"Find her," she ordered, and then repeated it more strongly. "Find her. You look upstairs, the children can look outside." Frustration that she could not go and search herself was evident on her face.

Rosie didn't understand, but her fear had grown, for this was obviously a serious matter. A part of her wanted Aunt Ellen to get away, if she were indeed a prisoner here, but another part told her that there was something wrong with Aunt Ellen, that she mustn't be allowed to do whatever it was they were afraid she would do.

"She's not upstairs," Rosie said in a quavering tone. "She came down a few minutes ago, while you were drinking your tea."

Neither of them expressed surprise that Rosie knew

whom they were talking about. Grandmother drew herself together, visibly gathering strength.

"Find her," she said urgently. "Go and look for her, everywhere. You, too, George."

And then she added a final command, one that, once it had fully percolated through Rosie's mind, at last began to make a few things dreadfully clear.

"She has the matches," Grandmother said. "Find her before she can use them."

17

THEY LOOKED EVERYWHERE, BUT they did not find Aunt Ellen, though Rosie found a few fresh prints of her high heels near the lilies of the valley. Ellen had torn up more of the flowers, hastily, so that some must have come up roots and all, for the earth was disturbed.

When they returned to the house, after looking around the barn and the rickety building that served as a garage and in a storage shed, and even at the little burial ground in the dense woods, Grandmother was waiting on the porch, her face anxious.

"No sign of her," Uncle George reported, "except that she was in the garden. Left tracks. I think I'll jump in the car and drive along the road, see if maybe she started walking to town."

"She knows better than to go where people will see her," Grandmother said. "She knows if anyone finds her, they'll put her back in the hospital."

"But she has the matches," Uncle George reminded her.

From what Rosie could judge, Grandmother didn't need that reminder. She was thinking of little else.

What, exactly, Rosie wondered, did Grandmother think she was going to do with the matches? What would Ellen try to set afire?

Luckily everything was still soaking wet from the storm. Nothing that had been rained on would be easily set afire today.

"Go ahead," Grandmother said after a moment. "But if you don't find her between here and town, come right back. I don't think she'll go where there are people."

She eased herself into one of the three rocking chairs and sat down, as if standing were too much for her, but to Rosie's relief she didn't look sick, as she had earlier in the day. After Uncle George had gone, she looked at the three youngsters standing before her, their faces sober.

"You might as well sit down," she said at last. "Chances are it will be a while."

Kevin and Nathan sank onto the top step. Rosie, after a moment's hesitation, took another of the rockers.

The silence stretched on for several minutes, and then Nathan said in his small, froggy voice, "The other chair's hers, isn't it?"

Grandmother sighed. For a moment Rosie thought she didn't intend to answer. Then Grandmother said, "You've seen her, haven't you? Talked to her?"

"Yes," Kevin admitted. Ophelia the kitten wandered around the corner of the house and leaped up the steps. *She must have escaped the upstairs room when Aunt Ellen left it,* Rosie thought. When Ophelia rubbed against Kevin, he began to pet her, absently. "This morning, while you were gone."

"I was afraid she wouldn't be able to resist taking a look at you. She was always so fond of your mother, and I made the mistake of telling her Rosie looked like Lila."

She sounded more sad than angry at either them or Aunt Ellen. Rosie dared to speak, too.

"She brought me the flowers in the night. At first I thought it was you . . . only she didn't use a walker. So we . . . went looking for her."

There. It was out, that they'd deliberately disobeyed orders to stay out of the east wing. Rosie waited, holding her breath.

Grandmother only nodded and set the chair to rocking gently. "I was afraid of something like this, from the minute you three showed up on our doorstep. That you'd hear something, see something, to make you suspect she was here. We probably should have just locked her in until you were gone. But she panics when we lock the door. George thought she was rational enough so that if we explained you'd only be here a few days, and that she must stay away from you, she'd do it. Maybe she would have, if I hadn't mentioned that you looked so much like Lila."

Excitement began to trickle through Rosie like electricity. Was Grandmother going to explain everything? Including, perhaps, why she'd given away her two little girls and never spoken to them again, until she'd called Aunt Marge yesterday?

"We thought Aunt Ellen was dead. We saw her tombstone," Kevin said, scratching behind Ophelia's ears.

It seemed an effort for Grandmother to speak. She had to pull herself together, muster the energy, each time. "Everyone thinks Ellen's been dead for years. They have to keep on thinking that, or the authorities will come and take her away again. You'll have to keep the secret. It probably won't be so terribly long, six months or a year, at the most, the doctor says. Although I suppose that seems a long time to you."

Rosie struggled with confusion. "She said she was sick, that she had to go to a specialist in Kansas City. Do you mean she's . . . dying?"

Grandmother's chest rose and fell in another long sigh. "She has a blood disease that will be fatal, sooner or later. She doesn't really suffer terribly from it, except that she's getting weaker all the time. I doubt if she'd be able to walk as far as town, even if she wanted to, and what she dreads more than anything else is being found out and taken back to the hospital."

"The mental hospital, you mean," Kevin clarified.

"Yes. She told you that, did she?"

"She said they locked her up, and she hated it. She ran away and came home. If she's still alive, though, why does she have a tombstone? Is anyone buried there?"

"Yes. Poor Sylvia. We didn't know it was her body when we buried her. She died in the fire, and we thought it was Ellen, you see. We had the funeral. I thought that was the end of it, the fires Ellen used to set. I thought it would be safe for my children to stay home. And then Ellen came out of hiding, and I knew it was too late for anything."

Grandmother spoke dully, and Rosie felt an unexpected twinge of pity.

"Do you mean you *wanted* them here? Mama and Aunt Marge?"

Grandmother's mouth twisted in a wry smile. "That's what everybody thinks, isn't it? That I sent them to Maude because I didn't want them, because I was too selfish to raise them. Well, and so they should, because that's what I intended. I couldn't tell anyone the truth, to make them think moving them to Maude's was only temporary. For all I knew I'd never be able to have them back, and I never have."

She closed her eyes, as if they hurt, and lifted a hand to massage her temple until Nathan's puzzled question made her look at him.

"What is the truth?" he wanted to know.

Rosie thought she had begun to guess at some of the facts, though she was confused and unsure. She spoke before Grandmother had a chance to reply to Nathan. "Who was Sylvia?"

"The truth," Grandmother murmured. She sounded very tired. "I've kept secrets . . . lied . . . for so long I'm not sure I even remember the truth."

Nathan's shocked expression made her sigh again.

"Your mother taught you to be honest, didn't she? Well, that's what I taught her, too, and that's one thing I did right, even though I couldn't follow my own teaching when the time came. Sometimes it's impossible to be totally honest, because if you are you hurt someone you care for very much."

To Rosie's horror, she saw tears form in Grandmother's eyes, though they didn't spill over. Mama had cried when Daddy died; otherwise, Rosie had never seen a grown-up cry, and it was disturbing. Everything, these days, was disturbing. She thought Grandmother had forgotten *her* question, but after a moment she started talking again.

"You asked who Sylvia was. Well, you know enough

now so that it probably doesn't matter if you know the rest, but you have to promise not to talk to anyone else about it. Lila taught you to tell the truth, so if you promise, you'll really have to keep still about what's happened here."

Rosie wanted quite desperately to know the whole story, but she wasn't sure she could make such a promise. "We might have to tell Mama," she said.

Grandmother considered that, rocking gently back and forth. "I suppose that's reasonable. She may have trouble believing you. It's such an unlikely story. Yes, Sylvia. Well, Sylvia was a girl who worked for us. A hired girl, we called her in those days. Today I suppose she'd be a maid. She was pretty, and young. She wanted pretty things, too, more than she could afford on what we paid her."

She began to rock perceptibly faster, and her chair made little *squeak, squeak* noises. "She was enthralled—you know what that word means?—with Ellen. We all were. Ellen was an actress. She went away to the city and worked on the stage, and on the radio for a while, and then had a few parts on television. I was only a little girl when she went away, and to me my big sister Ellen was beautiful and famous and she had money for things the rest of us only dreamed of . . . clothes, and shoes, and jewelry. She always brought presents for everybody when she came home, even after I grew up and got married and lived here on the farm. It was so exciting when she came."

Her mouth twisted ruefully. "Oh, yes, it was very exciting. Besides the glamour and the excitement of having an almost famous actress in our midst, things *happened* when Ellen was around. We didn't figure it out at first, but we had *fires* when Ellen was here. Little ones, which never got out

156

of hand because someone always found them in time. Once we thought Marjorie had been playing with matches behind the barn and ignited a haystack, though she denied it. We didn't punish her because we thought she'd been so terrified once it got going that she'd learned her lesson."

It was obviously difficult to tell this story, yet Rosie had the feeling that maybe Grandmother had kept it bottled up for so long that it was a relief, too, to let it out at last.

"And then Albert caught Ellen watching a fire he'd set to burn off the stubble in the cornfield; a wind came up and it got out of hand for a few minutes. The men came running with hoses and they stopped it before it burned anything but some grass, but in the middle of all that running around Albert saw the expression on Ellen's face. At that moment it was endangering some of the outbuildings, but she wasn't apprehensive, she was excited. That set him to thinking, after the fire had been put out, and when there was a fire in the broom closet off the kitchen he accused her of setting it. She denied it, but even I could tell she was lying.

"I was shocked and heartsick. I asked her how she could have done such a thing, and she said, 'I love to watch it, you know. It makes me feel better. It's so pretty.' And I said, 'But you might have destroyed the house, and my children were in it!' She looked at me then in a way that broke my heart, because I could see that she really couldn't help it, and said, 'I never thought of that, Dorothy. I was feeling so miserable because I didn't get the part in that show. I just wanted to see how pretty the fire was, so I'd feel better.' Can you imagine? Not thinking about the fact that she might have killed my children? And she adored both of them."

157

A cloud passed over the sun. An omen? Rosie wondered, not wanting to hear any more of this dreadful story, yet unable as well to stop listening. She felt cold.

"They locked her up," Grandmother went on. "They said she was a pyromaniac, a person who feels compelled to set fires just to watch them burn. She especially felt the need to do it when she was sad or disappointed. My beautiful, beloved sister Ellen was mentally ill."

Rosie remembered the big poster in the room upstairs and nodded without realizing she was doing it. Yes, Ellen had been lovely when she was young.

"They had psychiatrists and psychologists and doctors, and eventually she convinced them she understood what a terribly dangerous thing she had done. She was an *actress,* remember, and she wanted out of that place so badly. They finally believed her, and they let her come home. Albert didn't trust her, and he didn't want her here, but I loved her, you understand. I *wanted* to believe her."

The cloud was passing; sunshine once more flooded the yard, but Rosie was still cold. She had felt it herself, this morning up there in Aunt Ellen's mirrored room: the distrust. Aunt Ellen had tried to be charming and hospitable, but Rosie had been afraid.

"She came home, and at first she seemed fine. She went away, on an acting job, and after a while I stopped worrying about her. I thought she was surely cured and that she'd be all right."

For long moments Grandmother sat staring out across the fields beyond the garden, but she didn't appear to be seeing them. She looked so tired that Rosie wondered if she shouldn't be lying down, resting, as Uncle George had suggested she do before they missed Aunt Ellen.

"She wasn't, of course. She had been very convincing, but she wasn't cured. She came home for another visit, bringing presents for everyone. Marjorie and Lila were as enchanted with her as I had been as a child. Some gentleman friend, a producer who had promised her a part in the next movie he made, had given her a stunning watch, and she was so proud of it. She wore jewelry every day, and ridiculous high-heeled shoes, even when she was out in the garden. The children trailed her everywhere, and she encouraged them. Ellen always liked being admired, and she was very generous with those who let her know they thought she was beautiful and talented.

"Sylvia was working for us then, and Ellen brought her a watch, too, though it didn't have any diamonds on it. Sylvia seemed pleased with it. They liked each other, she and Ellen, and talked like friends rather than as if one of them was a servant.

"And then," Grandmother said, "there was another fire. Ellen swore she'd had nothing to do with it, but Albert didn't believe her. He had to rebuild the back porch and we never did use that corner room back there after that. It wasn't until he caught her taking matches upstairs, though, that he called the people from the mental hospital, and they locked her up again.

"She begged and begged me to get her out, but of course I couldn't do it. That time I believed the doctors, that she would probably *never* be able to stop being so fascinated by fires that she felt compelled to start them. It was all the more likely, the doctors said, because she couldn't handle the stress of being turned down for jobs, of seeing actresses she thought were no prettier nor more talented than she was getting parts she wanted."

"And then she escaped from the mental hospital and came home," Kevin said, anticipating the next words. Perhaps he, too, found it difficult to listen to this story.

"Yes. Did she tell you that? She sneaked home and cried for hours, pleading with us to let her stay, swearing she'd never look at another fire, let alone set one. I wanted to believe her, though I was afraid; I could see what being in that place had done to her. They wouldn't let her have her jewelry and her pretty clothes; nobody fixed her hair or her nails. And, of course, she couldn't take acting jobs, and nobody was taking publicity photos of her. I begged Albert to at least consider not sending her back."

Grandmother took a deep breath. "We argued for days about it, and Ellen was on her best behavior. She'd almost charmed your grandfather, too, but not quite. Sylvia was still one of her biggest admirers; she liked touching Ellen's belongings, once borrowed a necklace from her. And then things began disappearing, and Ellen thought Sylvia was taking them. I couldn't believe it, at first. Sylvia had worked for us for more than three years, and I liked her. Yet when the diamond watch disappeared along with the little things, and your grandfather caught Sylvia wearing it away from the house, we knew she was a thief. It was one more problem to deal with, when we already had so many."

Rosie forgot to rock, imagination adding details to Grandmother's story: the tiny diamonds on the watch, and the unknown Sylvia dancing with her boyfriend when Grandfather saw her wearing it.

Grandmother's voice grew harsh, in the way that Rosie

had previously taken to mean she was hard and unfeeling.
Now Rosie guessed that it really meant that Grandmother
was struggling to keep from revealing deep emotion. "We
sent Sylvia away. She was very angry and denied she'd taken
any of the other things. That same night," Grandmother
hesitated for a moment, "there was a terrible fire in the
east wing."

18

THEY WAITED, AS IF FOR GRAND-mother to gain strength. The squeaking of the rocker made Rosie want to shout for it to stop, but she said nothing, and the tiny sounds went on. Out across the backyard, steam rose from the wet grass as the sun warmed it.

"We were lucky to escape with our lives. Albert smelled the smoke and woke up first. He yelled that he would call the fire department while I got the children. They were sleeping upstairs, and I dragged them out of bed and told them to run outside. Then I went to get Ellen, who was sleeping in that room she has now, but she wasn't there. The room across from hers was an inferno; I didn't open the door because it was too hot to touch, and I could hear the flames crackling behind it. I knew if I opened that door, the oxygen would rush in from the hall and the whole house would go before the fire trucks could get here."

It was so vivid in Rosie's mind. She could see the scarlet tongues of fire curling out the windows, where the black marks could still be seen on the bricks.

"I screamed and screamed for Ellen, but there wasn't any answer. Albert came running up and dragged me away. He said if she was in that room it was too late, there was nothing we could do for her; and he made me go outside. Marjorie and Lila were standing out there by that spruce tree in the back—it wasn't very tall, then—in their nightgowns, terrified. We all thought the entire house was going to burn to the ground, except for the brick parts, but the firemen managed to confine the damage to the east wing except for one corner downstairs, and we eventually repaired that. Quite a lot of the roof had to be replaced."

Grandmother rested again with her eyes shut. When she reopened them and spoke once more, her voice was flat. "They found the body of a young woman in the burned-out room, after everything had cooled off. We thought it was Ellen. It was wearing her watch and one of her rings. We grieved for her, and we had her funeral and buried the body out there in the family cemetery."

Nathan was trying to understand all of this. "But it wasn't Aunt Ellen," he said.

"No. It was Sylvia. We heard that she'd run away from home in disgrace, because everyone knew she was a thief. As far as I know, nobody ever questioned it when she never came home again. Apparently she'd come back here to resteal the watch, among other things—we'd stored some valuables of Albert's mother's in the room where she got caught in the fire and died."

In the distance they heard the sound of a car. Uncle George, coming back?

"The day after the funeral," Grandmother said quietly, "I found Ellen hiding in the barn. She had set the fire deliberately, though as always she swore she never meant to hurt anyone. She'd only meant to have a *little* fire, and it got away from her."

The approaching car was turning in at the front of the house. Rosie held her breath, wanting to know everything, yet wishing it was all over. She prayed fervently that Uncle George had found Aunt Ellen, but even if he had, what would happen then? This was a story that couldn't have a happy ending, Rosie thought sadly. As Mama had said after Daddy died, life isn't always made up of lived-happily-ever-afters.

Grandmother didn't seem to hear the car. It was as if a dam had broken. Now that part of the secret had been revealed, the flood that had burst through was unstoppable. Nathan had slid along the top step until he was close enough to Rosie to lean against her knee; they took comfort in the touch, each from the other.

"Albert was so angry. He said they would lock her up forever this time, and it would serve her right. He said her fire-building could easily have cost us our children's lives, and our own, and I knew he was right. It wasn't safe for Ellen to be running free. I even worried, for a while, that she'd known Sylvia was in that room when she lit the fire, but she swore she was innocent of that. I think that was true, because the body was found in a closet, as if Sylvia had heard Ellen coming and hidden there with a bag of loot she'd collected. The family silver, things like that. And then she was trapped by the flames, poor soul."

Rosie wondered if this were only another of the things that Grandmother wanted to believe, or if it were true. She hoped Aunt Ellen hadn't deliberately set a fire in that upstairs room knowing that the hired girl was in there. What a terrible thing that would have been to do!

Grandmother's voice dropped so low that the children leaned toward her to hear it.

"Then Albert had the accident with the tractor," she said. "He was so badly hurt that for a few days I couldn't think of anything else; I spent all my time at the hospital, and Maude came to take the children home with her until . . . it was over."

The old car bumped slowly around the corner of the house. There was no one in it except Uncle George. Even then Grandmother appeared unaware.

"When Albert—your grandfather—died, the children were still at Maude's. There hadn't even been time to tell her the truth about the fire. Ellen had gone into hiding, because she was afraid that anyone who knew would feel the same as Albert did and that she would be locked away forever. Even the children didn't know she was still alive. I came home to an empty house, and I think I knew even then that it would be that way always."

The car pulled past them and into the ramshackle garage. A moment later Uncle George emerged and came toward them, his shoulders sagging.

"I'm sorry, Dorothy. I couldn't find her."

Grandmother sat very still. "I didn't think you would. She ran away, and she's hiding somewhere." The next words apparently were directed at her grandchildren. "She's so like a child in many ways. When she was a little girl, she'd hide if she thought our father was going to punish her. That made him angry, and the punishment was more severe that way when he finally found her, but she couldn't seem to learn."

Uncle George looked around at all their faces. "You've

told them about her," he said, astonished and at the same time visibly relieved.

"They talked to Ellen. She told them some of it herself," Grandmother said crossly, as if she had been driven to confessing against her will. "If they know she's alive, living with us, there's no point in telling more lies. Dear Heaven, how tired I am of telling lies!"

"Do they know . . . all of it?" Uncle George asked carefully.

"Almost all." The hostility, the defensiveness, had seeped away, leaving only weariness. "I didn't dare bring my children home, you see. Ellen cried and begged my forgiveness, and swore she'd never again be tempted to start another fire. I knew it wasn't true. She can't help it, something inside her makes her *have* to do it when the need comes over her. She pleaded with me not to send her back, because the next time they'd never turn her loose, and she wouldn't escape so easily again. They'd keep a closer watch on her.

"The thought of what it would do to her, to be locked up forever, was more than I could bear, you see. I could face the danger of keeping her here for myself, but I couldn't do it for my little girls. For a while I convinced myself that I would eventually be able to have them back, but in my heart I knew I never could. Because Ellen kept trying to get the matches, and whenever she laid hands on even a few, there would be small fires. I couldn't risk having my children in the same house with her, and I couldn't send her back to the mental institution. Because most of the time, you see, she was perfectly normal."

In the silence, a bird trilled in one of the nearby trees.

Rosie felt the ache in her throat that went with the tears in her eyes. "I think," she said thickly, "that you should have told Mama and Aunt Marge."

Grandmother nodded reluctantly. "Maybe you're right. But they were too little to explain to them at first, and they couldn't be expected to keep it a secret that their aunt who had supposedly died in a fire was still alive. Even when they were older, I was afraid they'd give her away. They had reason to resent her . . . and me, too. I couldn't really expect them to understand and forgive me. Ellen would have been held responsible for Sylvia's death, you understand. They might even have put her on trial, because except for this awful compulsion to start fires, Ellen is quite sane. Either way, she'd have been locked up forever."

She gave a small, bitter laugh. "In a way it's been almost as bad for her here, except that she's had her own room, her own things around her. She's been able to continue reading her scripts, to pretend she's going back on the stage. But she hasn't been free. We've been her jailors, George and I, making sure that she never left the farm unless we took her.

"When she got sick and we had to find a doctor for her, we went to Kansas City, where no one knew any of us. The doctor said she has a blood disease, one that will make her weaker and weaker, until . . . she dies. There's no cure for it, though medication has slowed its progress. Actress to the end, she pretends she doesn't have it, though she can't stop the effects of it. Just in the past few months we've seen that she's more tired; sometimes it takes all the strength she has just to go up and down the stairs. So I thought maybe it would work, that I could tell her to stay out of sight until you'd gone. We always keep the matches locked up and a

167

close eye on her, so we decided it would be safe to let you stay here for a few days, if we were careful."

Grandmother bit her lip. "Only we weren't careful enough, were we? I hadn't counted on her wanting so badly to see Lila's children, and I should never have told her how much you look like your mother, Rosie. She just couldn't resist coming to see you."

Uncle George cleared his throat. He stood at the bottom of the porch steps, resting a hand on the railing as if he needed the support. "Ellen's lonely. When we go to Kansas City, we always try to stay a day or so, take her places where there are people. But of course they're strangers, not people she loves, and it's not the same."

How different things were from what they'd imagined about Grandmother and Uncle George, Rosie thought. Was it possible that the same thing was true about her mother? Had Mama, too, felt it necessary to sign those papers authorizing someone else to look after them, maybe because she was afraid of dying, as Grandmother had been afraid of sending her sister to an institution?

Rosie felt a powerful need to see her mother in person, not just to get messages from her through Aunt Marge. She hadn't felt that she herself would ever give up her children, under any circumstances. Now she wasn't quite as sure about that.

"I long ago resigned myself," Grandmother said, "to the fact that my children will never forgive me. And also to the fact that as long as Ellen lives, I can't even ask them to. I owed so much to Ellen, you know. When I was a child, she was the one who bought me everything important I ever had. She gave me excitement and anticipation and more love than my parents had time for. I just couldn't do it to her . . . put her back in that place that drove her wild with terror. Not even if that meant tearing my own life apart."

Uncle George moved restlessly. "What are we going to do now, about finding her?"

Grandmother sat very still, and then she leaned forward and reached for the bars of her walker. "Well, she may come back to the house and sneak inside. Hide in her room, or even in the attic. We'd better comb the house first, I suppose, and if we don't find her . . . I don't know where to look. She has no friends left, no one to turn to for help. And no money."

Again her laughter was bitter, with no real amusement. "She couldn't even steal any from us, until our checks come. We used to be comfortably well off, but we've had to use practically everything there was to take care of Ellen's medical bills and to give her a good time when we left the farm. We kept thinking . . . it might be her last trip to the city, each time. We wanted her to be . . . happy."

No one else had been happy, Rosie thought. She felt sorry for Aunt Ellen, if she couldn't help what she did and she was always afraid; but what about everyone else? Mama and Aunt Marge, Aunt Maude who had taken on someone else's children to rear, and Grandmother and Uncle George who had been as much prisoners as Ellen was? It wasn't fair. Nothing was fair.

"I'll start searching downstairs," Grandmother said. "Nathan, why don't you come along and help me, in case I need a young pair of legs for a quick errand? I'll lock up every room after I search it, so that if Ellen isn't there, she won't be able to get in later. The rest of you take the upstairs—the attic, too, George—and do the same thing: Lock what you can to prevent her from getting back in."

Rosie and Nathan stood up, but Kevin remained where he was on the top step, his face stricken. "It's my fault, isn't it? I didn't relock the pantry after we took out the pails. If I'd locked it, she couldn't have got at the matches."

Uncle George shook his head and reached out to put a hand on Kevin's shoulder. "No, no, boy. It's not your fault. You couldn't have known what the situation was, and I was in such a hurry to get your grandmother to the doctor I neglected to take the precautions I should have. You didn't understand why it was important to relock the pantry after you'd taken out the berry pails. How could you have known?" He started up the steps. "Dorothy, are you sure you're up to this? The kids and I can search. Maybe you'd better just sit still and wait for us. I don't want you to have another spell."

"I just took my angina medicine," Grandmother said stiffly. "I'll be all right. If I'm not, I'll sit. Be thorough, don't miss anywhere she might be hiding, but hurry."

She paused before she entered the house. "We have to find her as quickly as we can. She still has the matches."

Rosie was breathing heavily as she joined the others for the search for Ellen, wondering what would happen when they found her.

19

THEY DIDN'T FIND ELLEN IN THE house. Nor in the garage, nor the barn, nor the charred remains of the chicken house. The latter place wasn't likely, for there was little left that would provide a hiding place, but Uncle George poked it apart with the shovel to make sure.

"She burned this, too. I suppose you figured that out."

Kevin could no longer control himself. "How have you stood it all this time? Just staying here, being a jailor! You didn't have any fun out of life at all!"

"Not much," Uncle George admitted. "But your grandmother did most of it, for a long time before I showed up. I came home after I retired from the sea, and legally I owned half the property. Albert always ran the farm, but we both inherited it from our pa. I didn't have any other place to call home, though I wouldn't have stayed if Dorothy hadn't wanted me to. That was when your grandmother got hurt, trying to stop Ellen from getting the pantry key away from her. I heard 'em and broke it up, and a shock it was,

171

I'll tell you, to find out that woman wasn't dead and buried after all. Dorothy had to tell me what had been going on, and I could see she needed help. She didn't ask me to help, you understand. She's a proud woman, Dorothy is. Shamed, too, maybe, because things turned out so bad, but proud. And stubborn. Too stubborn to give up and let them put her sister back in that home with the bars on the windows."

He gave up on the remains of the chicken house and stood looking around. "Blamed if I know where else to look. Doesn't seem as if she'd try to walk any great distance, especially with no money and no one to confide in. She's depended on Dorothy for such a long time; probably sooner or later she'll show up and make all her promises again, never to do anything wrong."

Rosie saw Kevin's throat work before he said, "But in the meantime, maybe she'll set another fire."

"She might," Uncle George acknowledged unhappily. "Right after that rain, things won't burn so easy. But give the damp a chance to dry out . . . oh, my. Neighbors got a barley field that just might catch fire if she was to make an effort. I wouldn't want that to happen. The farmer needs the barley, and his house is too close to the field to be safe. Come on, let's go back to the house."

He sounded, Rosie thought, as if he'd made up his mind about something. When they reached the back porch, where Grandmother and Nathan were waiting, she discovered what it was.

"The time's come, Dorothy," Uncle George said, "to give it up."

Grandmother looked as stern and unfriendly as when

they'd first arrived. "I don't know what you're talking about."

Uncle George sank into his rocker. "Yes, you do. I'm talking about calling the authorities to come and find Ellen and put her where she belongs. Where she can't do any more damage."

Outrage made Grandmother look as if she were carved from stone. "I can't do that. It would all come out, and they'd probably put you and me in jail, too, for hiding her all these years."

"Maybe so," Uncle George conceded. "But I'd rather that than have Tom Doyle's barley field go up in smoke, and risk his house and barn, too. Not to mention his whole danged family. It's one thing taking a chance on our own necks, living in the same house with that sister of yours. We don't have any right to put other people in danger."

For a moment Grandmother was unyielding, pure granite. And then Rosie saw her mouth quiver; for a horrible moment Rosie thought she was going to cry.

Grandmother's voice cracked. "I suppose you're right. Let's make one more try at finding her, though. Everything's too wet to burn, yet, so it's not as dangerous as if—let's wait until dark, anyway, give her time to come home. She's like a child when she gets hungry. Maybe she'll come home."

"We already looked everywhere there is to look here on the farm," Uncle George said reasonably. "If we didn't find her the first time, we won't find her by searching the same places again."

Grandmother said nothing for several minutes while the others waited, and Rosie wondered if it was because she couldn't speak. She had often been afflicted that way herself, but it hadn't occurred to her that it might happen to grown-ups, too.

"Did . . . did you look up in the attic? She hid one time in an old trunk up there. Did you look in that?"

"Yes. And down the old well, and in the root cellar. She's not in any of 'em, Dorothy. The police, when we call them, aren't going to take well to being told we waited until it was dark to get them on her trail. It'll make it that much harder for them."

Grandmother rubbed at her arms as if she were cold. "Did anyone go back in the woods, around the graveyard?"

"Yes," Uncle George said. "I remembered that time we found her sitting on her own tombstone, and I looked there."

It was then that the idea came to Rosie. Slowly, at first, and even when it was fully formed it took her a little longer to say it.

"Maybe . . ." she began, then stopped, because it was probably too far-fetched.

Everyone was looking at her. Uncle George gave her an encouraging pat. "What, girl? You got an idea, spit it out. We'll take any help we can get."

"You said something once about Albert—Grandpa—and you playing Huckleberry Finn and Tom Sawyer in some caves. And I think . . . Aunt Ellen mentioned a cave, too. Is it . . . is there a cave big enough for her to hide in now? Where there were violets in the spring? She loves flowers, and if there was a place there to hide, too . . . I mean, she's afraid to go where there are people, strangers, and she's afraid Grandmother will punish her for talking to us and stealing the matches. . . . She told us there was somewhere else she went, before she got so hungry she had to come home and she was caught, and she didn't say where, but it wasn't far away. I suppose it's a silly idea, but maybe . . ."

Grandmother sucked in a breath. "Those old caves! But they were closed in, weren't they, after your pa decided they were too dangerous for kids to get into?"

"Haven't been back there in years," Uncle George said, but it was clear that he, too, was beginning to feel hope. "Yes, Pa had them sealed, but that was over fifty years ago. They don't make too many things that last for fifty years, not the way they used to. By golly, Rosie, maybe you made a good guess. Anyway, we'll go take us a look."

He got up and reached for his cane, then paused to speak to Grandmother. "If we don't find her there, I'm calling the police as soon as we get back. We're not waiting until dark."

He didn't wait for a reply, but Rosie heard Grandmother's murmured response as the others followed Uncle George.

"Yes. Yes, we'll have to call them, I suppose."

"Come on, we'll drive back on the lane," Uncle George told them as they loped to keep up with him. "I'm too lame to walk that far. Used to think nothing of it when I was your age."

The car was old, but it ran well. Kevin was in front with Uncle George; Rosie and Nathan sat in back.

The lane from the barn out through what had once been cow pasture had been worn into the earth by heavy traffic in days gone by; by cattle and tractors and the feet of those who worked the farm, or played there. It went right

175

through the creek, with no bridge over it; Uncle George drove on across and up the far bank, then turned right. The track petered out, and Kevin got out to open a gate, and then Uncle George stopped and got out on the edge of the stream.

"I plumb forgot those caves. Had a wonderful time there until one of 'em fell in," Uncle George said, getting out of the car. They all followed him as he made his way down toward the water. "Pa discovered them when one wheel of the tractor went through and spilled him off; he got scraped up some. And then when he found out Albert and I had been playing in there, might have been inside when the roof caved in—well, he forbid us to go there anymore. And when Ma found out about it, she made him seal it up so we *couldn't* get in."

"Would Aunt Ellen have known about the caves?" Rosie asked, almost losing her balance on the steep slope.

"Oh, I reckon she heard us talking about them, one time or another." Uncle George caught his own balance with the aid of the cane. "Watch your step, here. Albert was a great storyteller. He was always recounting tales about the old days. I'd be surprised if Ellen never heard him mention the caves. Besides that, you're right about the flowers. I haven't seen any violets lately, but she picked some wild primroses only last week, and there's none growing close to the house. I sort of reckon I saw some on the edge of the woods last spring, so she'd have had to come back here somewhere. Only safe place, really, that the neighbors wouldn't see her, that she could get away from the house. Away from us. Sometimes she just seemed to have to get away from us." He sounded sad.

176

He stopped, looking around to get his bearings. "Ah, should be right along here, now. Looks like it's pretty much overgrown with blackberries, consarn it. Nasty barbs, they have."

He reached out with the cane to poke into the thicket. "Yes, it's possible, child. She might have found the cave when she was looking for wildflowers. See, there's a primrose right over there. The violets were down that way, as best I remember."

"How did your father seal off the caves?" Kevin wanted to know.

"Well, I think he used the blade on the front of the tractor to push some earth over the edge, and then hauled in rocks, too. Lots of caves in Missouri, you know. Limestone all over the place—that's what this ledge is, here. Thing is, the creek goes up and down with the seasons and the weather, and in all that time since Pa filled it in, the water could have washed away some of what he filled it with."

The creek was low now. The rocky ledge they walked upon was almost as good as a sidewalk, Rosie thought. Her heart was pounding again. What would happen if they didn't find Aunt Ellen here? Would the police be very angry, as Uncle George said, first that they hadn't known an escapee from the mental hospital had been living here for years and second that they hadn't been notified immediately when she had escaped again, this time from the house and the people who had devoted a lifetime to caring for her?

The creek babbled over a rocky bottom, so clear that Rosie saw minnows swimming. A frog leaped in at their approach. It was so quiet and peaceful out here. No one spoke as they followed Uncle George to the right place.

"Ahhh!" Rosie heard him sigh as he came to a stop, and she saw why.

There was a hole in the embankment, large enough for Nathan to walk into upright. Beyond the opening, reachable only by scrambling over loose rock and earth, the hole was black and forbidding.

Rosie stopped. Were they going to have to go in there?

What if Grandmother was wrong about Aunt Ellen being harmless except for wanting to set fires?

What if Aunt Ellen refused to be taken back? What if she eluded them again and returned during the night? What if she decided to set one final, stupendous fire, and burned down the house while they were all in it?

"Ellen? You in there?" Uncle George called out in a perfectly ordinary voice.

There was no answer.

"Come on out, Ellen," Uncle George coaxed.

Nothing.

Kevin spoke in a near-whisper. "What's it like in there?"

Uncle George made his way through the rocky debris with difficulty; several times he would have fallen but for the support of his cane. "I thought it was marvelous when I was a boy. It's actually a series of caves, one off the other, like a honeycomb. I think Pa only sealed off this front one, that his tractor fell through; I'm sure he never explored the whole thing, the way Albert and I did."

He ducked his head and peered into the darkness. "Umm. I'd forgotten how spooky it is."

It was spooky, Rosie thought, breathing more quickly.

She hoped Uncle George wouldn't want *them* to go inside and search. Yet she stepped up beside the old man and tried to see what was inside, the boys crowding close behind her.

It was Rosie who saw it, the clue.

She caught her breath. "She's here," she said. "Or at least she's been here."

Uncle George reached out with the cane and tapped at a patch of soft damp earth at the mouth of the cave. It was the only place tracks could have been seen, for the rest of the approach was of layered limestone. "Yes. Imagine, walking all the way out here in those high heels."

But it wasn't the heel print Rosie had seen. She felt as if her chest had constricted, making it hard to breathe, and the air that emanated from the cave seemed very cold.

"There," she said, pointing.

Their eyes were beginning to adjust to the inner dimness, and now the others saw it.

There had been a cave-in, and it was recent; where rock and earth had fallen, the dirt was still moist.

And protruding from beneath the edge of the earth and rock was a fresh spray of lily of the valley.

20

"SHE'S UNDER THERE, ISN'T SHE, Uncle George?"

Rosie choked on the words, feeling the hair rise on the back of her neck.

Uncle George drew in a deep breath, leaning heavily on his cane. "Looks like it, sure enough," he said, and he sounded as shaky as Rosie felt. "Oh, my." He shifted his weight off the cane so that he could use it to prod a mound of earth with the end of it, uncovering yet another proof that Ellen had come here. With a sick feeling Rosie recognized the blue and white box of matches.

Uncle George withdrew from the entrance of the limestone cave and looked around, sinking onto one of the larger chunks of rock in the jumble along the creek bank. "Oh, my," he said again.

Kevin licked his lips. "Aren't . . . aren't we going to . . . dig her out?"

Rosie still stood in the cave entrance. This outer cave was not very large, perhaps the size of the bathroom in their old

180

apartment, but there was a darker hole beyond the recent rockfall that she guessed was either a tunnel or another cave. She raised her eyes and saw where a great slab of the stone had come loose and fallen down.

Then her gaze settled again on the sprig of flowers, lily of the valley that had certainly been picked in Grandmother's garden only a few hours ago. Rosie felt strange and frightened.

"Maybe she's still alive," Kevin suggested, a note of urgency in his voice. "Maybe we could still save her."

"Oh, no," Uncle George said, shaking his head. "No, no, it's too late for that. Let me think, boy. My head is getting too old to deal with this kind of thing. Let me think."

They stood there on the bank of the cheerful little creek, and Rosie saw a fish swim by. There was a blackberry bush just to one side of the cave entrance, with dark purple berries fat and glistening, almost ripe; she could smell them in the summer sun.

They allowed Uncle George to think. It seemed to take him a long time, but no one interrupted him. Finally he drew in a deep breath and used the cane to help him rise from his rocky seat.

"Ah, it's time to go back to the house," he said. "There's nothing we can do here. Let's go."

Silently they made their way back up the embankment and got into the car. No one said a word as they returned to the house.

Grandmother stood up when they drove into the yard. She seemed older than when they had first come, Rosie thought. The lines in her face were deeper, and her mouth curved downward in an almost angry expression, but Rosie was no longer afraid of her.

"You didn't find her?" Grandmother asked as they got out and climbed the steps.

"We found her, Dorothy." Uncle George sank into his rocker as if his legs would no longer hold him up. "She went into those old caves, all right. The rains and all made the ground soft, I guess. The roof caved in on her; buried her. No question about it. Happened at least a few hours ago; the lilies she carried had begun to wilt, and the earth that came down had dried out a little on the top, though it was still damp underneath. I doubt if she even realized what happened; it must have been over for her in seconds. It was a very large chunk of rock that came down."

Grandmother's knuckles had turned white on the bars of her walker, but she said nothing. Her face scarcely changed, except that Rosie thought she compressed her lips even more than before.

"Ellen's dead? You're sure?"

Uncle George nodded. "I'm sure."

After a moment Grandmother sank back into her chair, staring out across the fields. "I suppose . . . what had we ought to do, George?"

"I've been thinking all the way home," Uncle George said. "Legally, Ellen is already buried out there with the rest of the family. There's a headstone to prove it. Sylvia's parents are dead and gone; nobody's still wondering about what happened to *her*. The caves are as good a final resting place as any. I can have the entrance closed in again, so that no one else wanders in there. It's too dangerous for anyone to explore."

Uncle George leaned forward and put his hand over Grandmother's on the arm of her chair. "Nobody has to know, Dorothy. We don't need to call the police. It's over."

"Over," Grandmother echoed faintly. "I knew she was sick—" She turned to the children as if appealing to them to understand. "She couldn't help the way she was. And she'd been so good to *me*. I had to do what I could for her." She turned back to Uncle George. "I've had the responsibility for her for so long. Now . . . I don't know what to do. I don't know how to *feel*."

"Let's not do anything for a while," Uncle George said. "Let's just sit and think about things. Maybe this way was the best." He looked at Rosie and Kevin and Nathan. "Sometimes living is harder than dying. I think it was that way with Ellen. And it's easier going fast than slow."

Rosie had such a peculiar full feeling in her chest, a feeling she couldn't describe. "We . . . we could pick the rest of the lilies of the valley," she said hesitantly. "And take them out there. Before you close up the opening to the caves."

Grandmother nodded. "I think Ellen would like that," she agreed, and groped for a hankie in her apron pocket. She dabbed at her eyes, sniffed, and pulled herself together. Rosie thought she must have had a lot of practice pulling herself together.

"When you see your mother," Grandmother said, "tell her I asked after her."

There was a moment of rather awkward silence. Aunt Marge wouldn't be able to forgive and forget, even when she knew the truth, Rosie worried. Aunt Marge felt so bitter. Was it possible that Mama, though, might not feel quite so angry at what Grandmother had done to her children, when she understood why?

Rosie didn't know. But she thought if it were *her* mother, she'd want to be told, even if it was years late. "Maybe," she said, speaking almost too softly to be heard, "you could call her, when she comes home."

Grandmother had to clear her throat several times. "Well, maybe I could, at that. If you'd let me know when she comes home."

"Only when we go home," Nathan said, pushing his glasses up where they belonged, "we have to go in foster homes."

Grandmother got that stern look. "You don't know about that yet, do you? You didn't stick around long enough to let the grown-ups who care about you figure out what to do. You sort of jumped out of the frying pan into the fire without even knowing if there was heat under the pan."

Nathan's chin dropped; his expression was uncomprehending. "Huh?"

"She means we did something foolish," Kevin explained, "without figuring out that we might be getting into worse trouble. I guess she's right. Only I hate to go home."

"We hate to have you go home," Uncle George said.

Grandmother didn't say anything to suggest she agreed with that. Instead, she said, "We're too old to raise children now."

Uncle George sighed. Old people seemed to sigh quite a lot, Rosie thought. She didn't know if it was because they were tired, or impatient, or simply resigned to things they couldn't control. "I guess you're right," he said. "But I'm thinking. We won't need the money to take Ellen to the doctor again. We could buy bus tickets with the money we had set aside for that."

"Aunt Marge is away until Saturday night," Rosie said.

"Well, you could go on Sunday then," Uncle George said.

That afternoon they picked all the blossoms that were left in the small flower bed. They went out to the back field, even Grandmother, who was stiff and remote and did not cry when Rosie placed the flowers in the mouth of the cave and Uncle George said the Twenty-third Psalm.

That evening Uncle George fixed chicken and dumplings for supper, which they ate in silence. Afterward they sat in the parlor and Grandmother let them look through the photograph albums. When they came to the pictures of Rosie and Kevin and Nathan, all she said was, "Maude used to send me pictures sometimes."

The next day they played around the house and in the barn, trying not to be in the way, though they no longer really felt unwanted. And on Sunday morning, Uncle George drove them to town and put them on the bus back to Summerville. Rosie's eyes brimmed with tears as she waved good-bye to him through the window.

Just before they reached Summerville, Kevin said nervously, "I'll bet Aunt Marge is going to be pretty mad at us."

Rosie thought so, too, but she didn't say anything. She was getting a cramp in her stomach from worrying. Not about Aunt Marge's anger, for that would eventually pass, but about maybe being separated from her brothers.

Aunt Marge met them, and she was as cross as they had expected her to be.

"It was a completely stupid thing to do," she told them

as they walked toward her car. "You put everyone to terrible trouble."

None of them answered, and she got in and slammed the door. "We were trying to do what we could to keep you from going into foster homes. If you'd stayed put and let us work on it, we might have worked it out and none of this would have been necessary."

Rosie tried to listen to the words without really hearing them. Perhaps Aunt Marge was right, but on the other hand, they'd done *some* good at Grandmother's, hadn't they? They'd met her and found that she didn't hate either their mother or themselves. They'd met Uncle George. And Grandmother was going to talk to Mama on the telephone when Mama came home. Maybe, someday, they'd even go to visit Grandmother and Uncle George on the farm again.

"Rosie, did you hear me?"

Exasperation was making Aunt Marge's face very pink. Rosie blinked and looked at her aunt. "I'm sorry. I guess I didn't hear you."

"I said, Mrs. Kovacs and I have arranged for a friend of hers to come in and stay with you while she's in Florida with her sister. Mrs. Limmel, from her church. The social services people have almost agreed to it, if it's all right with your mother, and why wouldn't it be? I'm going to the hospital to talk to Lila tonight, and it'll probably be a few more days before we know for certain. The thing is, if we get someone to stay with you, you'd darned well better behave yourselves and not pull another harebrained stunt like this."

"We won't," the three of them murmured at once.

Aunt Marge kept on talking all the way back to Mrs. Kovacs' house. Rosie stopped listening, or perhaps it was that she had found a new way to listen.

Underneath the anger, Aunt Marge had been worried about them. Frightened for them. Once she'd gotten that out of her system by yelling at them, she'd probably feel better.

Grandmother had shut everybody out for ever so long and hadn't allowed herself to love anyone. Grandmother really did care, only it was too painful, so she'd tried to convince herself and everyone else that they didn't matter to her. And now they had made a little crack in that wall around Grandmother, and maybe when Mama heard her voice—and the explanation that Rosie and Kevin and Nathan would already have given her—the pain that Mama felt would ease, too. And someday maybe they could be a happy family once more.

Aunt Marge turned into the driveway and switched off the ignition. "The first thing you'd better do," she said, "is apologize to Mrs. Kovacs for causing so much trouble."

Rosie was the last one in the house. She walked slowly because she had so much to think about.

She hoped Uncle George was right about dying sometimes being easier than living. At least as long as they were living, they could be working to make things better. They could hope for whatever they wanted.

Rosie couldn't wait for Mama to come home from the hospital so they could tell her everything.

The last thing Uncle George had said, before the bus pulled out, was, "Don't worry. It's all going to work out fine."

The last thing Rosie had said to him, called from the bus window, was, "We love you, Uncle George!"

Mrs. Kovacs grabbed her in a big hug as soon as she entered the house, almost crushing her ribs. "Oh, child, it's good to have you back!"

Rosie hugged her, too, and then she said, "I'm sorry you were upset, Mrs. Kovacs. But I truly can't apologize for running away, because we needed to do it. We met our grandmother and Uncle George, and we learned a lot of things we needed to know."

"I should hope so," Aunt Marge said tartly. She didn't know what Rosie meant, of course.

But she was getting over being mad, and when Rosie smiled at her, Aunt Marge reluctantly smiled back.

Uncle George was right about one thing, anyway, Rosie decided. Most of what she'd been worrying about was going to work out fine after all.